THE UNDERMINER

Hornito: My Lie Life

THE
UNDERMINER

OR, THE BEST FRIEND WHO CASUALLY DESTROYS YOUR LIFE

MIKE ALBO
WITH VIRGINIA HEFFERNAN

Illustrations by Carl James Ferrero
and Mike Albo

BLOOMSBURY

Published by Bloomsbury Publishing, New York and London
Distributed to the trade by Holtzbrinck Publishers

All papers used by Bloomsbury Publishing are natural,
recyclable products made from wood grown in well-managed
forests. The manufacturing processes conform to the
environmental regulations of the country of origin.

Library of Congress Cataloging-in-Publication Data has been applied for.

ISBN 1–58234–484–1
ISBN-13 9781582344843

First U.S. Edition 2005

1 3 5 7 9 10 8 6 4 2

Typeset by Hewer Text Ltd, Edinburgh
Printed in the United States of America by Quebecor World Fairfield

My Friend

My friend must be a bird
Because he flies.
Mortal, my friend must be
Because he dies!
Barbs has he, like a bee.
Ah, curious friend.
Thou puzzlest me.

—Emily Dickinson

CONTENTS

Bright Young Things

Campus of Clarkwell College, graduation in the town
of Clarksville, somewhere upstate, 1990

Hey there. Whew, what a day. First I did the Ellipticycle
for an hour and then I had to run to the Dean's small
cocktail party for Honors students and then I had to
hurry up and turn in that Green Form so I could
graduate.

You know, the Green Form.

The Green Form? You didn't turn it IN?! No, it's that
green form that we got at orientation when we first came
here four years ago. Yeah, sorry, but it kind of is
important. It's the Green Form. They told us never to
lose it, remember? No not the blue registration card, the
GREEN Form! Maybe you just have it in your wallet
and you didn't even know or something. Check it.

Wow, your wallet. You actually keep everything all
crammed in together like that? No, it's just kind of
amazing. I would freak out if I couldn't streamline my

wallet. Oh—I think you dropped this twenty. Oh, no wait, it's actually mine. Sorry.

Well anyway, you need the Green Form to graduate, otherwise . . . No, I mean I'm sure they have an alternative. You probably just have to wait an annoying day or one term or year or something. Wow, I can't believe you forgot.

You are so funny, you. Man, am I going to miss college and all your crazy flakiness. Ha ha! You've always been the funny one in our gang.

It's so sad how we're all going our separate ways, our little gang! The Clarkwell College Cabal! Sheila: the smart one. Tyler: the artist. Greta: the icy beauty. Sam: the actor. Me: the stable one. And you! The fun, funny crazy one! With all your plans and your spilling wallet and poetry writing and music and acting and whatever you have going on at the time! You're like the outsider of the gang. Not outsider-outsider. But I mean like, like Outsider Art. You know, like cute, sweet, weird. Like those artists who build towers in their backyard out of, like, TV dinner trays or who scratch the entire Bible into a bar of soap with their fingernail or who paint a mural of Imelda Marcos with chocolate pudding and end up in mental institutions. I mean like not obviously insane but more like all your efforts may not get you anywhere, may not be fully embraced by the public, but you're gonna just do it anyway, no matter what. And that's just great. You're like the outsider in that sense!

But I think what I'll miss most of all about college is working on staff at the *Loon*. It's too bad you never decided to work on the *Loon*. I feel like they totally would have understood your oddball sensibility there at that fun, scrubby, award-winning, risk-taking college humor magazine that has launched the careers of so many late-night talk show hosts and comedians. Whatever: politics. Everyone has to be so "cool" these days, you know? I'm really going to miss the *Loon* staff: Carson and Craig and of course Conan. I don't know, you never know who you're going to stay in touch with after college, but I know I'll stay in touch with Conan.

Meanwhile Sheila is already gone! Yeah, she just sailed through her LSATs and is spending the summer interning in New York City for some hotsy totsy star lawyer at this huge firm in Midtown. I know! It's amazing. I'm gonna miss her. She's nervous, but she has always been one of those people who barely has to study and just gets a 4.0. She's such a genius, which is such a godsend, because I had someone to hang out with since I had so much spare time too, since I can speed-read. She just *gets it.* Aw, remember how we would visit you in your favorite little nook in the library? Working so hard like a little elf!

What are you going to do tonight? Sheila's gone, and Sam's got a big audition tomorrow, so he may be down for the count too. Sam's so funny. He always gets so nervous and intense when he prepares for a part, you know? I hope he gets this role. Good old Sam, following his dreams of being a big actor! I mean I believe in his talent, but I guess I'll have to be there for him through the tough times like I always have with all his difficult auditions and clingy girlfriends. He gets in over his head with one of them, then he always comes over to my place, sobbing and sad wanting to sleep over . . .

Me? No! Not at all, not at all. We're totally just close close close friends. I'm just the person he runs to when he's sad or upset. Poor Sam—it's so weird to be born with magnetism. His otherworldly, robin's egg blue eyes, his Greco-Roman statue stature, his broad shoulders and dark, worn-in leathery voice. It's so weird how people treat Sam differently just because he is beautiful. Being so close to him, I've learned so much about how to deal with the lookism and assumptions people place on beautiful people. I think he sees that in me, you know? That there is someone who sees there is more to him? I mean we've talked about it. You know, how there is this mutual attraction, how we are so compatible. Almost too compatible. But I'm just not interested in him like that. Like you were.

No, it's cool. Who wouldn't be? Sam's like one of those rare beautiful souls. But you know, that is what makes him so desirable to people, because he is so vulnerable and sensitive. He's real: he burps, he gets a pimple, and he gets sad. I've seen him cry, with me, over, you know, one of his girlfriends, or just looking at a sunset.

God, watch Sam and me totally end up together! Wouldn't that be hilarious? No way, no way.

Ha! Remember how you begged me to introduce you? We would see him at Wollman Hall, and I knew him from my Beaches, Coasts, and Rivers survey class, and you would stand next to me in your funny baggy blue painter's pants you always wore, dying to meet him. And remember you would wait in the waffle line at breakfast because he always got sausage there, and you would get big waffles every morning just so you could have a few moments to talk to him? So cute. I think that is totally where you gained your infamous "Freshman 15," don't you? Man you were so goofy then. But cool!

It's so dumb how you two never got along. I think he was just stoned that night at the Frosh Mixer when he called you "the Tagalong." I mean, sure, you do get along now, after all that awkwardness.

God that was such a fun night. You and me and Sheila and Greta, remember? You were so drunk that night! Greta got so mad at you! Remember? We were in the basement of Pi Kap. They were playing "Shout" just like in *Animal House,* and everyone was getting on the floor, for the "get a little bit softer now" part. You were totally making out with some random person in front of everyone. Greta was next to Carl, and she and him were totally connecting, in a quiet subdued way and then—it was so funny—you literally pushed her out of the way and made out with Carl too, and then lo and behold you two started dating! No, just joking. But yes! No! Yes! You totally have to remember! It was such a famous night. It's fine.

I mean you told me yourself over and over how much better you are for Carl because of how passive he is. How he is almost frightened by Greta's sort of dark sexuality, and her unsmiling exterior. Greta can be pretty unapproachable for that. She's aloof. Not, like, panting for approval. That's why she was always so weird around you and Carl.

But of course you may still feel awkward around her. Just residual stuff from freshman year when you guys went to go see *Henry and June* and you pretty much locked her in your dorm room for the weekend, "experimenting!" Ha, ha! You were so intense! She was so not into it! You guys were so weird! Wow that was so long ago . . .

Narcissistic? Maybe, I mean in a way . . . yes I can see how you would think that. Intimidating? No, not really. Maybe if you have a low opinion of yourself. Greta just expects you to hold your own. She respects people who respect themselves.

By the way, have you even talked to Greta? No, I was just wondering. I mean I'm just wondering how you guys are with each other now. I mean all that is like ancient history, right? Right.

Just wondering.

Well anyway. Congratulations on your Folk and Myth degree. You concentrated on Florida Panhandle folklore, wow. I was so surprised you didn't get Honors since you tried so hard to be schmoozy with your advisor—I mean, I'm sure that's probably a good strategy. That's the way you get ahead in this dog-eat-dog world.

So what are you doing after college? Nothing yet, yeah. I know. It's hard to just dive into things and just shift gears. I'm not sure what I'm doing either. I know, it's so hard to choose the right path for you. It's like one false move and you may lead an entirely different life full of flaws and mishaps. Huh. Wouldn't it be great if there was, like, a pill that helped you chill out and make decisions? I know you would totally love that, right? Ha!

Well, if ya don't have a clue about your lifeplan, what are you doing this summer?

You got a job as an intern! Cool beans. Where? An art gallery in New York! Faw-faw! What gallery?

Bonwyck Gallery? Weird! Did they expand their program? I thought it was just for teens. No, I'm sure I'm wrong.

Speaking of art, did you hear? Tyler got accepted to RISD for grad school. Total free ride because they thought his work was "the best" and "showed the most promise" of all this year's graduates.

He hasn't told you? He probably didn't want to have you get upset and repeat all that interior drama that happened at his Senior Show. Anyway, whatever.

God, after college, I don't know what I'm doing either (Hello! Where is that pill? Ha!). But I did get this really weird call from some animated TV show that is starting up? It's got this really boring name, *The Simpsons*? I don't know it's probably dumb, but we'll see. "The Simpsons." So lame, right? Whatever. The Simpsons the Simpsons the Simpsons. How boring, sorry to bring it up.

The Simpsons . . .

Well, anyway, they offered me a job pretty much the day after graduation, so I won't be getting hammered drunk like you and your other "constant party" friends will be doing tonight. I have so much to do and I have to be clearheaded so that I can get up early, have Honors brunch, say bye to Sam and his parents (they are so, so nice; his dad is like the Mayor of Santa Cruz and his mom is the Director of Development of Universal, so that's cool), so I have to say good-bye to them, open my special ceremonial present of keys from my family (we have this dumb Nantucket beach house heirloom tradition when someone graduates, it's totally psychotic), go to this little Dave Matthews Band unannounced concert, and then pack and get on a plane and—

Oh, yeah. He's playing. It's an industry thing but I can
. . . probably . . . get you in. It's weird how I know him.
I mean, that time he just basically saw me in the crowd
and pulled me onstage in a total Bruce/Courtney moment was so long ago, right? He just felt the connection.
I love things like that. It makes me have faith, you know,
that people really do see your integrity through the
complications of life. So now we keep in touch and
he just showers me with concert tickets still even though
we never see each other because he is on the road and all.
Why don't you meet me outside of the F Level of the
Amphitheater, the D-23 entrance? You should just get
there and wait. I'll be meeting Sam and a bunch of
people to hand out tickets. If I'm not there, we'll just try
to meet up later. OK? God, sometimes I wish phones
were affordably portable or something so we could call
each other!

Gotta go! But definitely keep in touch. Bye!

CLARKWELL COLLEGE
STUDENT INFORMATION

Awards, recognition-----

Name+-----------
Address------------

Mother's Maiden Name
(for security purposes)

Major------------
Minor------------

Dorm------------
High School GPA--

This form must be presented at graduation for
Final Acceptance. DO NOT LOSE THIS FORM

Cool Days

open mike night at Kafka-fé, after band ''2 Much''
plays, 1991

Oh my God, I am so glad I got a chance to see you
perform. Wow that was fun! That was just fun! Really
fun! I got here right at the end, but I pretty much caught
enough to understand your whole deal. Sorry the crowd
was so small . . .

But they were all clapping. You really got a lot of
applause. Did you have a lot of family and friends in
the audience? It just seemed like everyone knew you or
something. Oh, you work here too? I guess that internship at Bonwyck Gallery ended, huh? Well cool for you.
At least the staff here is supportive. Well it seems that way
at least. The way they clapped for you. I'm so glad I got a
chance to see you perform! Wow that was fun! Really
fun! Fun!

Look at you and your outfit. That is a super pair of
pegged jeans. They're the trend right now, I know.
Trends are so interesting to follow, especially someone

cutting edge like you who's so hyper-attuned to the whole "Appearance Industry." The way you keep up with things, and spend your money on magazines. Like I know that for you, you need to be really good about skincare.

Unbelievable. Your singing voice is so different from your appearance. It's like when I close my eyes I would imagine the person singing was a sultry sexy vocalist from prewar Berlin, and then I open my eyes and there you are! Your big shiny American face!

I recognized some lines from our freshman year poetry workshop. Or at least the same emotions. You never let something go to waste, you. I love that about you.

So this is your band now. Cool, cool. "2 Much." Great name. Ambitious. Why not? Just go for it! I think there's a German band with the same name but whatever, you probably won't have to worry about copyright infringement. You're probably like not on the radar you know? I mean, your band is such a certain kind of band. With a specific niche sound. So you won't have to worry. And, anyway, now Sheila is studying entertainment law (she says she is so sorry she couldn't make it! She's having dinner with the CEO of

Geffen Records tonight!) and she says it's almost worse for young songwriters to copyright their stuff because it scares off labels. So if I were you, I wouldn't bother at this point.

Sheila? Sheila's good, Sheila's good. Even though she's at the top of her class in law school, she still finds time for her crazy ideas. She is busy working on some cockamamie scheme: patenting this idea to put up racks for postcards outside of bathrooms in bars and clubs. It's so dumb and simple. I know! It's so retarded! Well anyway, she is begging me to help out, and she said she will give me "points" in the company if it ever goes anywhere. But I mean it's so dumb it's not gonna go anywhere.

So are you still with Carl from college? That is so sweet that you guys are trying to work things out. Long distance, right? Yeah. Sometimes those actually work! No really! Sometimes they really do! Sometimes! How fun! Really fun!

Are you sure you don't use some of the lyrics from your old poetry? I just remember this one line from when we had class together—it's so stuck in my head because it was the time you were so in love with Frank Spitz, our workshop teacher? Before you sort of flipped out for Sam instead? He was married, you were a student, and he was really moral about it . . . wow were you over the moon about him!

Of course I knew about that! Well, obviously you are over the whole thing because you don't even remember telling me! You told me at the anti-apartheid "Divest Now!" poetry reading. Me and like twelve others. You were pretty wasted. All that cheap white wine! You were so flushed with feeling for Professor Spitz. It was so screwed up. Not to like lessen your experience but I've heard that he is totally going out with a student now. Not like you and him where it was all flirtation and in your head. They are actually fucking and he's still married. To someone younger than us who is apparently totally gorgeous.

Oh! You know who it is? It's that stupid girl we used to see in Wollman Hall. The mopey one who kind of looks like you and Kate Moss's lovechild? Ugh— so obvious of Professor Spitz to go for the model. He's so Mr.-Affair-with-a-Student. Well, screw him! What a jerk. You know, it's probably good he wasn't into you. Everyone needs to go through that first broken heart experience, right? At least you landed Carl, huh?

I remember once—it was either before or after you met Carl—you made me hang out after the Take Back the Night March so you wouldn't seem so alone while you waited for the perfect time to cross paths with Professor Spitz when he walked to his Peugeot. And you gave him your sestinas? I remember you showed me that one with the repeated line: "I would roll in a thousand shared needles for you." That's the line I remember. And it's the chorus of that one last song you played just now, the sort of "grunge rock" one—what you are probably thinking is your single, right? Yeah, it's catchy, totally sounds like it would be played on the radio—like K-Rock or Q-103. Because grunge rock is definitely gonna be around for a while!

Oh my God, can I just say—your guitarist is SO HOT. I couldn't stop staring at him! He is so hot and just electric onstage. He is going to go places! Wow he really adds a lot to the band. Charisma, I guess. He is SO HOT. What's his name? Jacob Fountainhead. That's his real name? Really? You think it sounds contrived. No. Actually I think it's beautiful. You should be more positive about something like that. Appreciate the beauty around you, you know?

You know, sorry to interrupt you but I have to tell you your sound kind of reminds me of this other really obscure band, No Doubt? They're from Orange County in California and have a really big following there with skaters and young kids. Their music's sort of the same as yours, but less . . . I don't know . . . sad? But it's weird how similar you guys sound, and how similar your names sound, even. No Doubt. 2 Much. Wow, if one of you makes it the other is pretty much doomed. The music industry is so ruthless, right? But I'm sure something good will happen! I am so glad I got a chance to see you! It was so fun! Really really fun!

Wait. I have an idea. Do you have a demo? I'll be seeing Sheila tomorrow and could slide it to her. I mean you could do it too, since you know her, but maybe it'll seem less desperate if I do it. Oh great you do!

It's on what?

Your demo is on CASSETTE? It's not on CD? I can't believe you even still have a tape player! Hello, it's 1991! No way—you just bought it? Can I ask how much? Ouch, that's major buyer's regret. Tapes are—oh well, I guess you take your chances. Well, let's hold off on giving that to Sheila, until you get it in a modern format. I don't think A&R reps even play anything on tape anymore.

Um, can I just offer one bit of constructive criticism for your band? I think you really should update your clothes. I mean the pegged jeans thing and your hair is cool, but maybe it's time for you to start dressing, more, like, adult. More timeless. For instance, if anything, you gotta stop wearing like those rubber bands around your wrist. I know you think it's cool and sort of "punk" but why not just invest in a couple good pieces of jewelry, you know? You will be so much more respected by the Powers That Be. You know, some nice clean trousers and new, clean shirts. A few good elements to add to your sort of scrubby look. Just spiff it up a bit!

Oh my God, you'll appreciate this. I was hanging out in this club, on just some obscure night like a Tuesday and this strangely strong woman with steely eyes wearing a torn vintage dress named Courtney played. She did a whole long unannounced set of music from this weird new album coming out and then afterward I met her and we just kind of clicked. Oh you've heard of her? She's big? Oh I am so out of the loop. Then after the club at five in the morning, me, Court, and her boyfriend, Kurt, went and got matching tattoos. Little stars behind our ears. They were such a wild couple. So fun to be around . . . but Kurt was kind of sullen. So pure, though. Such an artist. Not *trying* so hard like so many people desperate for attention in the music biz these days.

To be honest I wanted to follow through this time on a group tattoo because of what happened to you and me with the whole Kermit the Frog on a jet ski tattoo thing in Daytona our sophomore year? I know I have told you this before, but I really truly did want to get the tattoo— but after I saw your butt cheek I just realized I couldn't do that to my body. I'm just such a lightweight when it comes to needles. I know you were drunk so it didn't hurt, and that makes me feel better about it.

Anyway, this time it was more discreet and Court and Kurt were both beside me, holding my hand through the pain. Really grounding. Like a family.

Did Greta come by? No? She said she was going to try to make the effort since, you know, you have been sort of caught up doing your thing. I guess someone just told her about your little indie rock band. I wonder who told her.

You guys should just try to reconnect I think.

No, of course it's her that has been standoffish. I didn't mean it that way. But she was making the effort to see you and you know how hard that is for her. Especially since she knows that you think she's narcissistic and everything.

I know. But you said that. I was just telling the truth. Come on. But you said—

Well anyway, I'm meeting up with her later if you want to join. What are you doing later? Oh yeah. I guess you have to clean up. Send steamed water through the cappuccino machines and wipe out the coffee thermoses and stuff. Wow I totally remember having to do that for my job after high school! It was better since I did it in Rome, but still. Funny how it comes back. I should totally write something about being a barista—the torture of it, the annoying caffeine-addicted customers asking for "half-caf double caf mochacchinos," ha ha! Now there's a good name for a band: the Baristas! Ha!

Oh my God that is the perfect name I need for this script I am working on for *The Simpsons* (yeah, I'm still there!) where Homer joins a totally typical "grunge" band! The Baristas is perfect!

Yeah, I'm still at *The Simpsons*. Pretty much paying my way. Yeah, I'm just freelancing as a producer now. It's just when they need me, though. I needed some time to work on my own stuff, and the executive producer said, "Hey, no problem, let's just give you the space you need," and so I'm just freelance now.

Me? Greta and I are going to Crish Crash, probably. Crish Crash? You know, the huge huge rave happening tonight. It's probably why there wasn't a crowd here—

like everyone in the city under twenty-five is going. Tyler is meeting me. He is scouting for more models for his photo series. It's so great how Tyler has the confidence he needs to experiment and be free as an artist. I know you sort of have contempt for institutions, but RISD was good to him.

No I mean you said that once. Like when you didn't get in. Whatever.

They love his theories about how his mundane life is art and his off-center pictures of his messy bathroom and dirty dishes are kind of "anti-compositions." Actually a few galleries are interested, including Bonwyck! He's been taking photos of me and a bunch of us just sitting around in unmade beds, listening to CDs, cutting our toenails.

Crish Crash. You didn't hear about it? Weird. Yeah, you kind of have to know how to find it. And sort of know the right way to ask. Wait. Here's the address. If someone stops you at the door just act like you know someone—that's what a lot of people who show up uninvited do.

Maybe I'll see you there.

Live at
KAFKA-FE
104 W 4th st
INDIE ROCK NITE! WITH:
SUNSET OVER PARADISE
BABY BLANKETS
2 MUCH
LOVING TRUTH SCENE
INTERNAL RAIN
BAD HEAD CHILD
SUNSHINE TOMORROWS
THE SHITS
BLUES YOU CAN USE
HEE!HEE!HEE!
FREE PEACH SCHNAPPS SHOTS!
10¢ WINGS!
COME SUPPORT LOCAL MUSIC!
LADIES FREE!

New on the Scene

outside in front of Club Hush, for a film screening
party of *Kill Fee*, 1993

Excuse me? I'm sorry, but this is a private party and—

Oh my God. Hi! I didn't recognize you. Jeez you look so
different! Jesus Christ! This is insane. I can't believe how
different you look! Maybe it's me, but fuckin' A!

Well, something's different. I thought you wore glasses.
Or your teeth. Or are you using Pantene? Is it a make-
over or something? Did you go on one of those talk
shows or something? No it's just so drastic!

So you're still here. I would have thought you left by
now. I mean the party, not the city.

Are you sure you didn't get a haircut? It looks different. It
just seems fluffier or something. Hm? No, I don't wash
my hair anymore. I just rinse it. At first it was dirty, but
then it became cleaner than if you use shampoo because
if you think that shampoo cleans your hair, it doesn't.

Shampoo is full of bleach and detergents that permanently strip your hair of important oils and then in a few years you experience aggressive balding.

So you came all dressed up for the film premiere party! That's so cute because if you knew this scene you'd always really dress down. We're probably just jaded.

It's insane in there. I'm working for Scorsese. You know, he secretly bankrolled *Kill Fee*. Anyway, I'm just helping them out with publicity and packaging. I've just been here since five so I'm leaving early. And I'm waking up early to go on a ten-mile bike ride and need my sleep. I'm a morning person.

Hey Uma! Hey Ethan! I'll be right over!

Are you here alone? Trawling around the film scene, huh? Right right. Trolling around the film scene. Trawling trolling around. Yeah, everyone is clamoring for a part of the indie film pie. This is sort of a weird party for that, but . . . you know, maybe you'll get a chance to show off a script to some hungry producer, or at least sleep with one! Hah! You crazy, funny weirdo!

Were you invited to the screening or were you just invited to the afterparty? Oh. Well, Sam was amazing. He just looks so luminous on film. His role in this I think is going to put him on the map as "one to watch." But no worries, I'm sure he'd still be friendly to someone like you.

Greta was here! She couldn't handle the crowd. You know how she is. She just likes to connect with people one on one. By the way, how is Carl?

You did?
    Aw, wow. I'm so sorry.
    I'm sorry you're dealing with that. Oh that sucks shit.
    I sort of saw that coming.
    No I mean.
    Anyway, sweetie, really? That must be such a world of hurt for you.
    To have seen it coming.

Lenny, hey! The band is warming up now.

Are you OK? No, I mean I know you say you are, but, really, are you OK? Really? Yeah. No. Yeah. I understand why you aren't sad, why you can't really show your emotions. I mean those kinds of things just play out, and that's what you guys did. There's nothing to be sad about. Take it slowly, don't ignite your fears. I mean maybe you're not feeling upset because your body is in a kind of indecision about how to handle the grief. I'm sure you've heard of Disorder. "D." There are totally mild forms of it in lots of people. Anyway, there are lots of options now for treatment of "D." Zoloft, Prozac, Askalar—just to help you through the bad patches of life.

I don't mean that you look like you need it. I just don't think it's a bad idea. And it's so hard to get over college hang-ups. I remember you telling me how you and Carl were like the nerdy kids in your dorms and that's why you got along. Which sounds like a really sweet story. And also sort of wrenching once things change. I guess nerds grow up and change, and some become not-so-nerdy and don't need the same nerdy things.

Isn't he like in London or something? Studying furniture design? Greta told me.

No, no, I guess they sort of keep in touch still, even though you guys don't. Nothing dramatic. You know, remember, they were really close all through freshman year before you grabbed him I mean pinned him down I mean started dating him.

No, whatever! Don't kill the messenger! I'm just telling you they are in touch, I'm not like, a part of the whole thing, you know? It may be hard for you to believe right now—with everything being so raw for you. And you probably can't see other sides because you are still feeling the rawness of the breakup. But people of the opposite sex can just be friends.

Hm, I guess I would be a little freaked out too if I heard that my newly-ex-boyfriend was in touch with my still beautiful ex-friend from college. Or maybe I would if I had your "head first" kind of personality, reacting before you've thought things through, with your poetry and openness for that kind of florid emotional world. It would make me tired and exhausted, but it's great that it's your way. It's adventurous. I mean, even way back then you were, like, feeling you couldn't survive without a boyfriend. I was just making a wide network of friends, getting the most out of my studies. It's sort of why I stayed a free spirit in college so I could really find out what and whom I wanted. I just didn't really want a relationship until recently. Now I finally feel ready to give myself to someone. In a mature way.

His name is Nicholas. He's, well, he's a lot of things. A teacher for Teach for America, he went to Harvard for American Studies but right now he's trying to get his helicopter license. But primarily he's an international DJ. He's remixing Sade's album right now. I'm so proud of him. He grew up in Southeast DC, in a disenfranchised community, and has really made something of himself. So I have been traveling around a lot with him. He lives in Harlem, and I stay there on the weekends. Getting into the beats and vibe where it originated, you know? He's been working on his own music, getting a demo together. But I don't need to tell you how hard the music industry is! Well, if you think it's hard for you, imagine how hard it is for a Person of Color!

Excuse me, can I see your pass? You don't have one? I'm just kidding, Mr. Lynch . . . It's me! Ha! Yeah, coffee soon . . .

Speaking of, have I got a wild story for you. Since I've been hanging in the scene uptown, you know, in Biggie's studio, or just chillin' with Chuck D, I've had a chance to open up to them in ways I never thought I could with other peeps. A lot of my friends up there: Rza and Jay-Z and Busta, they say there is something about me, that actually I may be black. So I started doing research and found out that my grandmother on my dad's side was a prominent Native American Leader so I'm a sixteenth Cherokee (which explains my strangely prominent cheekbones I guess) and then I found out that my great-grandfather on my mom's side was a freed slave. So they were right! I am a Person of Color!

It makes so much sense. Not only because of my incredibly curly thick hair and a good sense of balance and beat, but I mean there's just this special connection I feel like I have with a more tribally truthful way of living. And since I'm half black, you know, now I really get to explore the sides of me that have been oppressed by the culture and media industries. But I miss all of them. I've been traveling so much.

God . . . look at all these people standing outside trying to get in. It's so weird. Freaks me out. Just the palpable difference between the Haves and Have-nots.

So you're living downtown? I hear it's so expensive and built-up there now. I'm living actually in SoFoFi. SoFoFi? South between Fourth and Fifth? It's this sort of little-known enclave of amazing old factory loft spaces. I'm actually in the building where *Rent* was inspired. There are a lot of artists in the building. And it has a history of housing some of the most influential creators of our time—from Bernstein to Midler to Puff Daddy "Sean" Combs. I have the room on the roof with a beautiful view and cupola. Actually Sade's manager got it for me.

And what kind of music are you listening to these days? Oh, yeah, Nick Drake. Wow, I haven't listened to him since my depressed college phase. I'll have to pull all his albums out. Thanks for reminding me! Do you have that on tape too? (Ha ha! Remember your whole tape cassette demo fiasco?) Maybe your Nick Drake sounds "warmer" that way or whatever. Hmm. No I'm just suddenly remembering that Sheila's been looking for music for a series of commercials she is producing. Nick Drake may work. Thanks for the tip.

Oh my God, did you see Jacob Fountainhead on Conan? He really cleaned up his image. He is so HOT. I mean I totally spotted him as having star quality when I saw him playing with you, but now it looks like it's true. Wow, he was amazing. You think it looked dumb? Well the crowd was going wild. I know you have a whole thing with him but he's just plain talented. And guess what. Tyler is designing his CD cover. Ever since he won the Pricely Award for Promising Young Artists, he's got all these people begging for him. And what about you?

You're taking a trip? Trajanja? Yes of course I've heard of it! The small communal hard-to-get-to island off of Belize? I went there last spring. Be sure to say hi to Rogelio. You won't miss him. He is pretty much the social maven of the island. He's so "cursi"! He will take one look at you and decide whether you are cool or not, and either make your trip amazing or a kind of hell! Ha ha! No, it's probably not a big deal that you're white. You know, just be yourself. And since I'm sure you got your shots. Oh. You didn't? Wow, I wish we'd talked before. I'm sorry but yes, those shots are kind of important. Without them you really have a high risk of developing a lot of long-term stomach problems and you don't really get to leave your room. Yeah, you could try to get them today, I guess. I mean apparently they don't really "kick in" for like a week, but . . . yeah, you could try. Maybe they have made some medical advances since last spring.

Oh well, it'll be nice to rest.

Oh. It looks like they're opening the party to the general public. You could check it out! It'll be crowded but you know, you may as well just check out the whole deal.

Why are you shivering? God I hope you're not coming down with that terrible flu before your trip. Here, take my scarf. No, it's OK. You can give it back to me later. I think it looks good on you anyway. It just cleans up your style. And you know how I am always badgering you to stop wearing those funny pants and ironic clothes. It's more grown up.

Listen I have to go and get to bed, but you take care of yourself, OK? Maybe you shouldn't go in. Save your energy for your trip. Sleep is a good way to ward off those ruthless parasites. Don't go slutting around all night. Go home and take care of yourself. I worry about you, you crazy thing.

HANDWASH ONLY BY SCARF SPECIALIST. HANG LOOSELY IN COOL, DRY, REFRIGERATED ROOM. 100% CAYENNE AND HONEY-DYED BURMESE SILK.

Single in the City

at a French bistro, 1995

You're here early! Oh my God, do you have my scarf? Did you bring it?

Oh. *FUCK*. That's . . . OK. No. All right. That's OK.

No, it's just that I got it in India when I went there and it's just like this really beautiful thing and I really treasure it. It's just really important to me. It's not like that cheaply made Barneys Co-op stuff you buy. I don't mean YOU buy, I mean "you buy." Aw, I wish you had remembered. No, no, that's OK. You're so flaky sometimes!

Wait. Are you sick? You look sort of tired. Is there something wrong? Oh, you went out drinking last night? It's so great how you can still do those college things. You're so crazy!

Did you throw up? No, no, I just smelled throw-up for a second.

So, I have some huge news. I didn't want you to hear it from someone else, but guess what? I just made two million dollars from my book deal. Yeah, yeah. So, I'm pretty happy about it; my agent's pretty happy about it. Sheila's really happy about it because she is engaged to my agent! Ha!

It's just really lucky because you know how the economy is totally booming right now but experts are saying it won't last forever, and that you really only have this small window of time to make money or else you will be poor forever. So, it's like I made my money before the downfall, and I'll be able to live comfortably? It's kind of just "locked in." It's weird for once just to feel calm and comfortable about your life and retirement, you know what I mean? Well I mean you can kind of know what I mean.

And I can't talk about the details of the deal, but if you could just do me a huge, huge favor and just don't mention it to anyone? I know how you kind of have a problem keeping secrets! No just joking I'm joking I'm joking. You do though. I'm joking, I'm joking. You do though. I'm joking I'm joking I'm joking but you do!

Bonjour, monsieur. Nous sommes prêtes à commander. Non, pas de vin pour moi! Mais peut-être pour mon petit copain!

You're having a Bloody Mary? No. I'm not drinking anymore. I'll just have a simple peppermint tea.

Une tisane à la menthe, s'il vous plaît.

No, go ahead and go for it. Don't let me stop you. I've just realized there's a little more to life. But go ahead, have fun. You're so crazy!

So what's up with you? Have you seen Sam or Tyler? No? Yeah. Yeah. I don't know what the deal is with you guys, or what your scene is with those guys, I just don't want to get involved in that whole "war" between you guys. Hm? No, nothing. They haven't said anything about you. And if they did of course I wouldn't even listen so I wouldn't know.

Oh my God, when was the last time I saw you? This is weird but I am totally hanging out with the guys who invented Yahoo. We jokingly call it the Millionaire's Club. It started out as a joke, but now it's becoming important, you know? Kind of like what you tried to do with your band, "Not Much."

What? Oh, sorry: "2 Much."

We have a little dumb weird Investors' Club . . . just to kind of play around with some money. For instance there's this one that is just dumb that we are putting money in, just for fun. It's this weird Seattle-based coffee company. I can't remember the name. But the coffee is SO GOOD. But you know, since you're just starting, if you were thinking of putting away some money just for something solid, you should go for utilities. Something safe, concrete. Like Enron. You should invest in Enron!

The tea here tastes weird. Wow, where did you read about this place again?

OK, I'll tell you. You know that children's book that I wrote just really fast for no reason, *It's a Funny Sunny Day*? Well, apparently, who knew, it's selling like crazy and can barely stay on the shelves. So the publisher is begging for a three-book series.

And I just got another voiceover gig! It's so funny. They just like my voice so I don't even leave my house, I just call it in. I don't know how it happened, I just sort of fell into it. You should try it. But it's really hard to get into. But you should try it!

You're looking for a place? Well, good luck. God, it's so hard to find a good place right now. Don't wish I were you! This guy called me and begged me to take his beautiful four-thousand-square-foot loft space. It's three hundred dollars but actually he's paying me to live there forever. It's called an "infinity lease."

So what is up with you?

I think your body looks good, it's *normal*. It's a normal body. People get too hung up on thinness. You're more like a typical American.

But I know, like, when you are single, which you are, you can just get so self-critical. It's just so hard to find someone worthwhile. I count myself lucky that I found Nicholas. I could not even face the world if I didn't have someone by my side. I know you are sad about it, but it's cool to be single in some respects. Not having someone in your bed every night. The freedom you must have to wake up and go to the bathroom and drink alcohol by yourself. I always think of you as my simply single friend.

No of course you have had your relationships. With Carl, and others that were relationships to you like with that TA at Clarkwell and stuff. But blah blah, you should be proud of yourself! You are single!

Oh that's weird, because I just ran into Carl. Carl and I just had a really, really, REALLY good time talking . . . Yeah, he lives here now. I'm surprised you haven't run into him. You know, when you and Carl were going out, I never really understood why you liked him, but now I totally do! He is so funny and smart! I guess I mistook his initial shyness for being an asshole or just lazy.

No, he looks really good. He's good, he's good. Got his degree in furniture making and has already wrangled all these celebrity clients. He's been working out, taking kung fu. His body looks AMAZING. Yeah, he said he hasn't talked to you. He seems like he's just moving forward. I mean, you guys broke up and he moved in with Greta and he's getting on with his life.

Oh . . . I'm sorry. Did you not want to hear news about them? No you just seemed so silent suddenly. I just don't want you to get all overcome like you did when you saw them together at Jacob Fountainhead's show last spring. Wow was that a dramatic time for everyone. No! I know you keep saying you're over it. That's so cool of you, the way you are so resilient. Anyway, they're fine, I guess.

To tell you the truth, they are a little boring! They never go out, never want to make plans, they just want to spend all their time all over each other. And they just bought a huge beautiful place upstate and they're fixing it up together. Actually Tyler is up there right now. They commissioned him to paint a mural on the wall. Of course, with what's going on with Tyler's career it'll probably be worth more than the house! Did you see that amazing cover article about him in *Artforum*? Jeez!

Actually you didn't come up in conversation that much, weirdly. But Carl did mention how happy they are for you and your things and projects and efforts you have been working on. And they are both really glad that you aren't upset, and they wanted me to be sure you got help if you needed it. They were worried about you last spring when all the shit hit the fan, so to speak, and you got kind of . . . erratic on the phone and everything. Greta really wants to talk to you, you know, make contact. Take your time, take your time. But any time you want to talk, call her. She's at their country house upstate most weekends, working on her memoir.

I know you think Greta is narcissistic, but she's been through a lot. I mean the kind of childhood she had . . .

Yeah, she sort of came to terms with it recently. It's weird how things are at a positive confluence for her—Greta may have been the stereotypical gorgeous beautiful "bitch" when we were in college, and I know during the breakup, you screamed to Greta how she always manipulated people to get what she wants, but it makes sense. Not that I am condoning her actions, per se. But she had to protect herself growing up, and put herself through school. She's overcome a lot of obstacles, which kind of demands respect, right? Even though I can totally see how it might be hard from your perspective. I don't know. Greta's just been through a lot. Some people try to gain the nobility of hardship, you know? They move to the city with dreams of being rock stars or filmmakers or whatever trying to grasp at authenticity. And for some other people, it just shines through, naturally.

Anyway, Greta's much more open now, and she's really worked a lot out in therapy, which is why I think she wanted you to get your shit together. Also she took a short course of Askalar and it really helped her step back and reassess. Yes! Askalar. It's really helped a lot of people through bad patches in our modern times. She was diagnosed by her doctor as having Disorder and so they put her on it. Carl has been so supportive and understanding. He's such a caring great guy.

So they're fine. I mean you know, taking it slow and really careful about everything, but fine. Even though they are finally together, after all that's . . . been . . . um . . . between them, they are taking it slow.

I just thought it was best for you to hear all that from me, rather than, like, some awful random person.

So nothing's going on with you?

Ha! No, sorry. I was just remembering this joke that Carl told me. Go on. No, I'm listening, go on.

You got a dog, wow. How cute. What's its name? Checkers, that is so sweet. It's so important to learn to care.

Where did you get her . . . him?

At East Side Pets?! Oh wow. No it's just that place has such a rep as a horrible puppy factory. I hope he's had all his shots and everything. Oh really? Oh. Wait. Sorry, but you know what, I have to make a really fast phone call but keep talking.

Hi, Sheila? Hi! Oh wait. Hello? Hi, where are you? That's hilarious.

No, sorry, keep talking. Isn't it crazy, mobile phones?

Oh but it's always so crowded there. I'm kind of "in proximity." You know, just here with our Funny Friend. Hahahaha. No totally!

What did you just say? No, keep talking. I can totally pay attention.

Don't worry. Anna is a really close friend of mine I can get in there.

No keep talking!

What? Meet you where? No tell me again?

No keep talking!

Hahaha!

Keep talking!

Hahaha!

Hangover

brunch, the morning after, 1995

Hey! Wow! You made it. Did you like write it down on your hand or something? No it's just I swore to myself and everyone at Rio's last night that you were definitely not going to make it here so we wouldn't have to save you a seat for brunch. But come sit, no biggie, everyone left so there's plenty of room. No, go ahead and order something. We closed out our check though so don't try to do one of your little scams! You rascal! I'll stay for a bit. At least till you get your usual Bloody Mary or five!

I can't believe you are even standing after last night. What a night, huh? Aren't you hung over? Do you even remember how you got home? I'm glad you're OK—

Or are you?

You know I can never tell with you. You're so mysterious. You're so lucky you can always just get up the next morning and plow through the day like a tank after partying so hard! Also, wait. Were you wearing like some kind of padding or quilted type of underwear last night? Oh, I don't know. It's just at some point when you were flashing everyone it looked like you were wearing something white and absorbent.

No? Oh, weird. I guess I just thought I saw it. No! It was funny! Everyone was laughing. It was quite a night. Quite. A. Night.

So . . . do you remember what transpired or no? Well, you really made the night memorable. After you ran up to the coatroom and puked on Sam's things, everyone was saying how much they enjoyed last night. It was like "old saucy New York" where anything can happen!

Sam? Yeah, he was mad—you know his usual overly moralizing grudge stuff: "I never want to talk to that little fuck ever again," blah blah blah. You know how he is.

But I am glad you are here alone. I just wonder if maybe you may need some time and headspace and I wanted to talk to you about that. I mean Askalar helped Greta so much get over her time and—

No, I know you don't have anything to do with Greta. I am just saying maybe an incident like last night is just a little marker about how your chemicals are off, you know? And you are dulling some simple chemical imbalance. Some lost brain synapse that could just so easily be mended with some serotonin encouragers? At least that is the way Greta described it so beautifully in her National Book Award–nominated memoir, *Mending My Mind: Travels with Disorder*. Wow, how that took off, huh? So well timed. But anyway, you should totally try it, I mean, what's the harm, you know? It's not gonna stain you forever or something.

Oh! That reminds me. Sheila wants to know if you are going to keep that jacket of hers you used as a vomit mop last night. She said it's totally cool. It's just a Marc Jacobs coat and she just wants to know.

And whatever about this, but I think it may be a good idea to send a thank you/apology kind of note to Costas, the maître d'? He was just so patient and helpful last night. Especially during the whole "googoo-gahgah I'm a baby in a diaper" moment.

Yeah, you did. But like I said it was funny!

Ugh . . . but actually more seriously I should tell you that I got stuck having to defend you to a group of people all night. It was kind of uncool. They were talking such trash about you and I was like your main defender . . . No one big. Just Sheila, Alfredo, Alfredo's friend Joanna, Tyler, and a bunch of people from Miramax. It was awful. I mean, all that party pleasantry aside—I'm actually a little miffed about the whole thing. That's such an unfair position to put me in. And I've had to do it so many times. I don't think you know how much people—not "hate"—but really are concerned about you.

Actually I can't deal with you getting randomly emotional now. I'm really upset about it.

I'm sorry. I don't want to be an asshole about all this. Why don't you just have some water and chill out and then maybe write your apology notes. Things will get better.

Also, to boot, um, I totally don't mind if you don't thank me for getting your back last night.

No! Absolutely not! I will not accept any money! No, nononono. It was like seventy-five dollars. Because the driver was so angry he had to go all the way out to your place and then back into the city to drop me off, so I had to kind of bribe him. But nononono I don't want any money. It was more of a pain than anything else. Just buy me a drink sometime.

You owe me.

Are you depressed? You seem depressed. Are you depressed? You're chewing weird. No don't worry, don't
worry. I am sure Sam and Sheila and Miramax will totally
forget all about last night. I personally in a way think it's
cool. You single-handedly put some intrigue and life and
gossip into this tired scene! I mean we're all so aloof and
reserved and everyone is so accomplished and profes-
sional and sort of "set" now, and we are all craving for
someone to come along and just shake things up . . . give
us some scandal, you know? Ha ha! But no we were all
psyched. Whatever, you know?

Oooh. I have to go. Nicholas is picking me up to go see
some tap dance performance he's workshopping with his
friend Savion. Yeah! I know, he's a genius.

Here. I know you are going to kill me but this is some
information about Askalar that I got from Greta. She says
that from her research this will tell you all you need to
know about the relative safety of this drug. A bunch of
people thought you'd be a really super candidate. Just
look it over, OK? I swear that's all I ask . . . not for me,
but do it for you . . .

Askalar™
For problems with Disorder

Nervous. Fatigued. Disillusioned. In Debt. Tired.
You may be suffering from D—Disorder.
Now there is something to help with D.
It's called Askalar.

As opposed to days past when medication was only given to those facing steep and severe challenges, the little clear pill works for young, active, healthy people. If you've felt fatigued, thoughtful, or bothered by things around your face like your bangs, Askalar may be right for you.

What is Askalar?
It's a side-effects-free dietary supplement that simulates the production of Humansleek, a natural hormone that increases bloodstream angelica. FDA approved.

How can Askalar help me?
Here is a brief list of guaranteed effects:
- Helps eliminate stress, fatigue, and depression
- Boosts your immune system
- Makes you feel and look younger
- Makes you however thin you want to be

Is this for me?
You definitely need to take Askalar if:
- You are over 23 years
- You often feel tired, sort of tired,
  or you just say "I'm really tired" a lot in conversation
- You feel that your immune system needs help, but can't exactly
  put your finger on what's wrong
- Your memory is becoming weaker (Here's a test: Quick - What's the
  name of your third-grade Music Appreciation teacher?)

Askalar is available in thirteen doses of pills, sprays, or injections.
Important: drink seven full 8-ounce glasses of water with each dose.
Ask your pharmacist or doctor to tell you more about Askalar.

Natural Health

a chance meeting at Jasper's Yoga Studio, 1996

Excuse me, I had my mat here, and I—

Oh, wow!

Ha ha, hi!

I am so sorry I didn't recognize you in your tight workout clothes. Wow. You are practicing yoga now! Wow wow. Amazing!!

It's just so great how yoga has spread its influence across the four corners of America. Old people are doing it, fat people are doing it, retarded people are doing it . . .

Is this your first class? Congratulations for showing up. You know, just do what you can do. And if you get tired you can always just rest in child's pose. Do some gentle head rolls and rocking to warm up your spine. Me, I always like to warm up my hands.

It's just so weird that you're here! Isn't this place great? The purple waterfall and glen of bamboo and ferns. Is this your first class with Jasper? How did YOU hear about it? Oh, no I just didn't think he was advertising or anything. It's just weird.

Oh, yeah, he's an amazing teacher. He really works with your body's natural rhythms. He is so flirty. I bet he lured you in here with his amazing presence. He's so funny. Ha ha ha! We've been going out for a while, since he opened this studio.

Where's Nicholas?

Wow I guess I haven't seen you for a while. He um . . .

He passed away.

Six months ago. I am so blessed to have friends to support me and see me through such bad times. It was a terrible time for me. Oh, thank you, thank you. I appreciate that. Yeah. It was a painful, painful sick accident. But I've made my peace with it. Hm?

Um, well, to be honest, I would really rather not talk about his death? Pardon my bluntness but it's really actually none of your business? I hate to sound all dramatic but could you, like, respect my privacy?

No no no! Of course I know you didn't mean to be nosy, of course of course. It's just been really hard with him being so well known, dealing with his estate, and all his recordings and master tapes of this weird girl group that he thought was going to hit really big called Destiny's Child—all left in my possession.

Hey Christy! No take my Yoga Nidra tape as long as you need it. I don't need it back anytime soon.

Hi Willem, how are you? Sure, I'd be happy to give you some pointers. Same place after class, OK? See you then.

Sting. Happy Birthday. Bengala Nataraj.

Hm? Yes that's him, that's Sting. Um, but see, here in Jasper's studio, fame is something we leave outside the door with our shoes. I would just keep that in mind. OK? Relax your eyes. Meanwhile I will relax my hands and stretch them out. They are really killing me! Ouch!

Oooh. Does your neck hurt? I can just tell. I think you are definitely a Weeshta.

Weeshta? It's part of the Ayurvedic system? I studied it in India when I was there. Of course it is a much more vast modality than this but essentially there are three types of people into which we learned all humans can be divided:

Shpashta—long, thin, naturally toned bodies, problems with small pores and emotional generosity, occasional soreness in the hands, from having them too open all the time, trying to offer themselves to the world.

Oooch! My palm really needs to be stretched out today!

Vashtas—muscular, rough, dark people who are strong and unusually attractive. They have problems with their pecs, eyes, and biceps. Also they tend to get overly devoted to people, but once things go wrong they are quick to hate. Like Jasper or your ex-boyfriend Carl.

And then there are Weeshtas—who tend to have, um, wider body types. They are the people who usually need drugs and socially sanctioned "life-helpers" like Prozac or Askalar. And they tend to have loud voices and problems with gas, skin eruptions, allergies, rashes, psoriasis, flaky eyebrows, seasonal affective disorders, depression, digestion, alcoholism, drug addiction, attention disorders, social acceptance problems, public place panics, family conflicts, twitching anal canal syndrome, bulimia, body dysmorphia, acid reflux . . .

And sore necks!

But these three modalities are all really equal. It's Eastern, so it's not about any hierarchy.

After Nicholas's passing I went on a soul-quest. I traveled for a month with just a backpack and a sheaf of paper, and after trekking through Nepal, I found myself at a beautiful temple in Drakkar—an isolated village in the Simoom valley. The temple was nestled in the side of a white cliff, covered with vines. I walked into the vast central altar area, and I was eerily alone, but there were lit candles and the smell of *nag champa* wafting through the air. I hadn't really cried until then, and the tears for Nicky flew out of me. I was sobbing and sobbing. Then I felt a hand on my shoulder, and suddenly felt an overwhelming sense of . . . how do I put this in a Western way . . . of joy. Inexpressible joy! I turned around and there behind me was an old, old man smiling down at me with the kindest face. He gently gestured to me to rise off of the ground, out of my pool of tears, and to follow him. And that old man was Sahatma Yoginanda. He is the last living master of an ancient form of Ayurveda. He is 120 years old, and on his last phase of life on this plane of existence. "You know why you are here," he said to me. I said, "Yes, yes I do," because I kind of did know that my life had been leading to that moment. He led me to a chamber of libations, and anointed me one of his disciples. Along with about four others, he had selected me—to learn the special nuances of the Ayurveda. So I began studying with him, and learning this ancient craft of healing and self-knowledge. You can find some of the teachings in the dampened-down forms of Western "New Age" and astrology.

Like for instance . . . you're a Gemini, right? Do you know the rest of your chart? Just tell me your birthday and I will tell you. I have the Ephemeris memorized.

You are a Gemini, with an Aries in VENUS??? AND a Weeshta? Oh my God. That's random. No, it's nothing. But this will be a perfect class for you because Jasper is going to read a series of Rumi poems about the long, long road to finding love, which is a very "Aries in Venus with Weeshta Conjunction" issue. But you probably know that.

Listen. Um, I know this is embarrassing, but if I were you I would have wanted someone to tell me a long time ago. Your breath is kind of stale.

No! Not all the time, but sometimes. I know, it's so embarrassing but really it's not that big of a deal. I just thought you should know. I would be so angry at a friend if they let me go for months without telling me that I have had bad breath, and I'm just an honest person. It's probably a Weeshta digestion issue. Maybe you could, like, keep an apple in your bag to, you know, clear out your palate. You should like eat an apple.

Keep an apple in your bag!

There. Perfect. You can think about that while you practice "Cleansing Breath."

What? Shh! Class is starting!

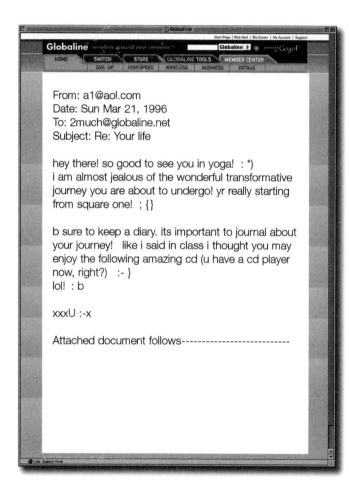

In a secret place inside each of us burns a magnetic fire of creation, the Shakti, waiting to rise up and change our lives.

For those of us on the Weeshta path, this fire can sometimes be blocked by intestinal buildup and feelings of envy.

presenting

Weeshta SHAKTI !!

This is your chance to get this gorgeous album, specifically designed for those on the Weeshta Path, before it hits the stores in a couple of weeks.

This record is a celebration of the body in its fullness. The Weeshta Full Moon body: the waxing, weighty, earth-bound, dirt-centered body. This compilation album offers an extraordinary journey of listening and healing as masterful musicians evoke, celebrate, sing, and play to the same vibrant spirit of the ecstatic longing of the Weeshta soul as it constantly cries for escape from its earth-bound form.

"Each song is a perfect prayer for inner peace for spirituality's neediest cases ... rising on rich rhythms and serene, soaring vocals ... a joyful dance into the divine heart of compassion."

— David Aura (reviewer for cdnow.com)

The Artists Include:

Bhagava Deva
"Cosmos for Dummies"

Jai Jasper
"Curing Feelings of Longing and Lust Through Touch"

DJ Sabbah Sibbi Sabbah

Shamana
"Make my heartwords sing!"

Includes:
- Vibrating songs to help with digestive trust problems.
- Encouraging words from Sphasta and Vashta leaders to help you with your Weeshta feelings of searing yearning and envy for others' life paths
- Humorous interludes by **Sark!** and **Squish,** the Weeshta mascot

The Fat Flush '90s

in the foyer of a friend's renovated brownstone, 1997

Oh my God, hi! I was just leaving! Hi, hi, what are you doing here? I didn't know you still were friends with Sam! Oh, that's right. He says you're on his list serve. I forgot.

Well look at you with your new haircut! You've had it for a while? I guess I haven't seen you! Well look at you! You got a haircut! It looks really different! It's a haircut! I like the way it frames the circle shapes of your face.

Wow, what a house, huh? Sam used free-trade mahogany wood. I am so happy for him and his amazing success. I mean, the Ten Hot New Actors article in *Vanity Fair* and then his first hit Broadway show. Wow. I am sure Sam would totally love to see you. And introduce you to his new girlfriend, Cameron, this amazing actress who is blond and gorgeous with great comic timing to boot. Oh, you've heard of her? Cool. I just can't tell who is "known" and who isn't anymore. I barely pay attention. You more like read that tabloid crap, right?

No I know it's fun so you can see parties and whatever. Oh! Could you hold on a second?

Andy! Andy! Hold on a second I'll be right there.

Are you here with anybody? No? That's fun that you're your own person and came anyway. It's all good. It's all good.

Do you want me to hold your bulky coat while you get straightened up? Oh. That's not your coat. That's your— more your sides, I think.

Oh no, there's totally people left in there . . . it's like at that point of a party where people are just coming to desperately hook up, you know? Ha ha! Of course I should let YOU know—the bar's in the back! And there's plenty of your favorite—bourbon! Drinkie drinkie!

What? Oh you don't drink anymore. That's great. God, end of an era, good for you—congratulations. That is so . . . I'm so proud of you. Is something like this party hard to go to for you?

Andy! I need to be here for a bit. Could you get me a mojito? I'm just thirsty for something liberating and delicious. Thank you so much!

Sorry. That's my friend Andy. He's so fun. He's a stylist. He's just distant and intimidating around people he doesn't know. He's actually totally nice once you get to know him. So you haven't been drinking, so you probably aren't going out as much. That's probably why I haven't seen you. You have all your sober friends and support groups and stuff. You know, I have a confession. I hate rigidity. My friend Adam just wrote the most interesting well-researched piece in the *New Yorker* about AA. How the whole sobriety culture can be like worse than alcoholism. No, seriously, in some cases. But no, I know, you were really a different scenario. It's different for some people, like you, who needed it, since it's something organized.

I mean it just made sense, because the last time I saw you, you were kind of . . . well, you were sort of . . . well it just looked like maybe you were beginning to see the shape of the problem. The Void.

When was it I saw you? Oh I know, it was at yoga class last winter. Are you . . . um . . . not going anymore? Ooh! That's right! You injured your neck! Ow! Ow!

Yeah, I think Greta told me that someone told her about that noticeable swelling thing you had. It looks like it's kind of—no, I mean, it's not swollen, it's just puffy. It could just be the overhead lighting. Huh. It's just so important to put padding under your neck for "shoulder stand." I always thought you were kind of doing it wrong.

You know, just get it looked at. I mean, I'm sure it's nothing. But you should get it looked at. Yeah.

Hm? No, I don't go to yoga anymore. Actually I practice Pookalan now. It's an ancient mystical health practice that's only known to like fifteen people in New York.

It's sort of the source to a lot of Westernized, tainted traditions. It's sort of hard to explain but it's about release from delusions. You know, not being so caught up in busy lifestyles and superficial "party" yoga. It's about not being "out there," but being "in here." I'm "in here" now. But you've kind of always gravitated to Western modalities or been in extensive therapy so you probably are more Western. And, remember, you're a Weeshta. Weeshtas are very Western, steeped in Western oils. "Supersized," you know? It's exciting.

Debra! Debra! Hey Deb! How are you? I know! Let's blow this joint! This party is so dying down we have to get outta here! Did you see Andy? He's right over there . . .

So there is this guy in there, who you will either be in love with or *hate*. His name is Jonah and he looks a lot like you before you filled into your adult body. But he's younger than you and he is doing SO WELL with his career. He just got a regular part on *The Sopranos* and he's like twenty-four years old. He's a friend of Sam's. They worked on the new Coen brothers movie together. I don't know—it's like he's more sincere? I don't mean that in a bad way about you at all . . . I more mean that in a generational way, like we're these cynical Generation Xers and the people younger than us have promise?

Did you see Jacob Fountainhead was here? With his A&R rep who is actually cool and not a jerk? Jacob's so funny and successful now? With his album deal with Virgin and everything? Do you not keep in touch with him?

He came zooming in from his SNL appearance to just say hi to Sam. He's been a really big supporter of Sam's work since I introduced them—I mean, you know, Sam is so covered with people trying to be his friend or trying to microwave old friendships with him that he sort of appreciates someone kind of "screening" people for him. And since Jacob is such a close pal of mine . . . you? Right, yes I remember you used to work with Jacob. Where did you guys work together again? That's right, Kafka-fé. Oh weird—that was so long ago—

Andy! Be sure to tell Deb about the afterparty!

Sorry. Oh, yeah it's this stupid small afterthing we're going to. It's just a stupid and small afterthing.

Oh no, Uma is meeting us downstairs. We don't need to call her.

It's dumb . . . it's small . . . a stupid . . . afterthing . . .

Anyway, yay about that little play you wrote and performed! I didn't see it, but Jack said he saw it. So, yay! Great! It's really great that you are doing that. You did it, you took a step. You know I really admire you. It's just so great that you are just going to stick it out and see how long it takes.

And with TV and film being deluged with money, it's so great how you are sticking with theater. It's just so honest. You know I should really tell Conan or a producer or someone about it. Oh it closed? Well let me know next time!

Oh wait! Do you have it recorded? Maybe we could give it to Sam to give to his producer friend, Harvey.

You have it on what? VIDEO?

Oh my God for real? That's like the new 8-track. You should you know invest a little in your future and fork over some dough to get it on DVD. It's just so much easier. No one watches tapes anymore. But you know . . . it's all good. We spend so much time in life doing what we do, learning. Look at it this way: if you were always doing something that you loved you probably wouldn't love it.

It's like this argument that Meyer Shapiro made in the fifties about the Modernists. What? Shapiro? Oh my God, that's beyond so interesting that you don't know who he is. Anyway—no, I'm not laughing, I'm just—it's just that he's like the preeminent art critic of the twen-tieth century—no, of course, I'm not like: "Ha ha, you don't know who he is." I mean, there are so many things you DO know about from your Folk and Myth major in college that I don't know anything about, like that amazing Ndembu Indian custom that you always bring up in conversations with new people we just met? No, no, I'm not saying that, I'm just kind of astounded. Shapiro. Anyway. It's all good. You just don't bury yourself in books like I do, which is great. You're not a reader.

Well now you're sober so you'll have PLENTY of time . . . Oh! Do you have an extra Altoid? You don't? I just heard something joggling around in your pocket.

Oh, it's your Askalar. Oh wow I've never seen that kind of Ascalar pill before!

Well good for you. I am so sorry, but I really have got to bolt!

Andy! We've got to hurry! We still have to pick up Jacob!!

Sorry. You know, I have to say, you look really grounded.

Andy!

Like you're really more solid now, more in your skin.

Andy!

You were kind of always, you know, sort of "wacka-wacka"—like running around all over the place or whatever—but you seem so solid and substantial now. It's like you're a really big fat person spiritually, a really solid individual! Is Askalar really helping? Well great then. I have to say I am so glad to hear a positive story about that drug to counter all those reports out recently. About how it numbs your creativity, adds permanent water weight, etc.

OK. Have fun at the party! It's sort of dying down now but I'm sure you can still Get Your Freak On! See you later!

Askalar™ For problems with Disorder

ALL PATIENTS SHOULD READ THE REST OF THIS MEDICATION GUIDE

One month's trial based on recommended retinologies with total dosage of 13 sprays and injections.

Stop using Askalar and tell your provider right away if you:
- Have symptoms of intolerance
- Start to feel sad or have crying spells
- Lose interest in activities you once enjoyed like shopping or cable TV.
- Sleep too much or have trouble sleeping
- Become more irritable, angry, or aggressive than usual
- Have feelings of worthlessness or inappropriate guilt

DO NOT
exfoliate, excoriate, suddenly inhalate, breast-feed, overdose, or think too much about any-one.

ASKALAR CAN CAUSE
Abdominal area problems
Bone and muscle problems
Hearing problems
Shortness of breath, hives, swollen face or mouth, red patches, or bruises on your legs

Askalar has less serious possible side effects.
The common less serious side effects of Askalar are dry skin, chapped lips, dry eyes, dry nose. If you wear contacts, you may inad-vertently rip off your corneas. Sometimes the Disorder may get worse for a while. You should continue taking Askalar unless told to stop by a prescriber. Askalar may also cause uncom-fortable blood, brittle whiskering, dizziness, blinking, fatigue, or blurry vistas that smear

like when you are on a subway going underground, and other noticeable moments like that subtle dread you may feel at work as you stare at the asthmatic laser printer wondering if there is any kind of forward movement in your career, or when you watch television and observe a talentless loser warbling out forgettable pop hits and raking in more cash and happiness than you ever will, or as you see yet another couple with tinted hair and stupid, blank, dance beat eyes who dress like reality show contestants from Miami and marvel once again at love's dodging randomness. And then when you think you have taken your lumps and God or Karma or the Faerie of Life owes you big time, you will walk into another party where there are thirty people dancing pathetically to some old club music crap like Technotronic and think to yourself, "Jesus Christ this is such a lame party, but maybe this is the night I finally fall in love" and you stand next to the sweaty cheese and chalk-dry crackers and some gangly grad student you are barely attracted to starts up a conversation and you think "I'm least expecting it this could be the One," and then the ugly motherfucker starts talking about his fiancé who is in De La Guarda and she walks up with her blue-black Argentinian hair and you suddenly feel the need to prove you are just sexlessly interested in Art and Expression and overcompensate by having a darling and intense conversation with her and then two hours later you are in a cab alone suppressing a series of roiling upchucks from the cheap red wine, and you think the world has become some foreign and loud amusement park that seems wildly rewarding and amazing to everyone but you.

Active ingredients: Probiotin and Humansleek, beeswax, butylated hydroxynanside, edate disodium, soybean oil flakes, FD&C Yellow No. 6 and titanium dioxide.

From: a1@aol.com
Date: Sun Mar 21, 1997
To: TomEEE2000@aol.com, Saddleburn@hotmail .com,
shaktibomb@nyr.rr.com, tuckerCARLSON@inch.com,
hanleysean@aol.com, sweetkitty@earthlink.net,
2much@earthlink.net, cybersnack@condenast.com,
lndyboy@freeware.com, Vidyalankara@hotmail.com,
Freeformjazz@centerforlearning.org, rentavibe@godiva.com,
victorbingo@tropicana.com
CC: lilrudi, lippylonglegs, Latinbiker, urbanproductions, medi-
apolis, scatterbot, jamarr, georgEENAA, galoore, sonhouq,
markmark, mike.milley, photonica, PEGGEENOONAN, ohula,
uhura, corona, glibby glap glooby, nibby nabby noobie,
midgidiboola, bibbity bobbity boo.com.uk and britneytits.
Subject: DOCTOR FAUST

Hi guys
I'm afraid there's a virus going around called DOCTOR
FAUST. It tends to attach itself to your hard drive and wipes
out all your memory in seconds! While I don't have the virus
myself, a lot of people I know are losing all their records,
watching helplessly while their important spreadsheets, novels, screenplays and Quicken accounting are blipped out of
existence before their eyes!
　I hate to sound like a witch hunt or something but one of
the people I have CC'ed above not only HAS the virus, but is
spreading and infecting others at a horrible pace. After extensive research, my intern Bette has narrowed the possible
infectors to the above list. Bette says that the virus is most
likely coming from someone with an email they haven't
changed since they were 25, and may have the number "2"
and the letters "M" "C" "U" in their address. Whoever you
are, I hope you'll apologize to everyone. This is pretty major.
And I strongly advise you all to check your systems and run
Norton Disk Doctor for the offending infection.
Meanwhile, I'm including photos of me and my boyfriend
Ben meeting Prince William in London! Hilarious! (he's actually really nice!) Xxxxxx U.

Art Stars

at Bonwyck Gallery, 1998

Thanks so much for coming! That's so nice of you to come. But wait. Forgive me but I kind of think I didn't invite you . . . I mean by accident, because I just sent invitations out to a few select—

Oh that's right you used to have an internship here at Bonwyck . . . before I became Board Chairperson. That's right. Before the big '90s art boom, right right. Simpler times.

Ooop! Hold on—

Mary. Thank you so much for coming. We'll talk tomorrow. I am so glad you're interested. Tyler should be here any minute! You know how he is, fashionably late!

Huh. I didn't recognize you. What's the cane for? You have a hernia? What a bummer. Wow and you're so young for such an injury. Wow. It's funny I thought the cane was fake. Like it was one of your crazy fashion statements . . . you making your big entrances like you do! Like that time you wore an adult diaper. You didn't? I thought we all decided you did. Oop! Hold on—

Hi Ghostface Killah! Sup! Thank you so much for coming! How goes it? How's the new record coming? Great to hear, great to hear.

What kind of surgery did you get? On which side? Well, you may as well keep the cane handy because you know what they say. It's just that Ben my boyfriend is a doctor and if you have a hernia on the right side you are almost certain to have one on the left. If you have a flaw deep in your chromosomal makeup, that makes you susceptible. It's just weirdly inevitable. Like if you have sinus allergies you're susceptible to facial aging. Or if your first love ended badly, you will repeat the tragedy over and over. Or if you lean toward cocktail consumption, you're bound to get throat cancer.

Are you okay? You seem weird. Do you want another vodka tonic?

Have you seen my boyfriend? I wonder where my boyfriend is. That's weird my boyfriend was just here a minute ago. Where is he? Ben, my boyfriend? My boyfriend Ben? Oh there he is!

Oh look who's here, pooky, pooky poo. It's Ben. Benny Wenny woo woo. Ben honey bun? I don't think you've met my old old old old friend. My oldest friend in the universe. Ben, this is—

Oh. All right, no, of course your patients are the priority, of course, go ahead. I'll be here till ten, and then we'll meet up at Da Silvano and go home. OK, kissy kissy moomoo.

He's on call. He's a little stressed. He's actually heard a lot about you and knows who you are.

Don't you just love Tyler's work? It's so "post graffiti." All those late nights he spent with Chinese and Latino gangs in the Bronx, tagging subway cars and power plants while other people took the typical road of internships and jobs at coffee shops. He's genius. With work that is robust and energetic. The biomorphic curves of graffiti in new emotional ways. Figurative and abstract simultaneously. So serious and informative of our culture's loss of community. Tyler's is a sacred art. I know how you kind of looked down at Tyler's work in college, but—

You didn't? That's funny. I thought you did. I know he was always kind of angry about what he perceived to be your criticism. But he appreciated it in his own way. He causes such visceral reactions. At least that's what the *Times* review said!

Oh you should totally read it. I'll email it to you, or ask Bette to do it.

Sweetie, can you email—

I'm sorry. I can't believe I am saying this but how do you spell your name? I've just gotten so clogged with names lately. Right—

—can you email Ty's Times review to . . .

What's your email address again? Is it still your old band? It's different! Wow, welcome to the millennium! Ha ha. What is it? Soconfused@prodigy.com—well, that's cheery! Well I'm glad you changed it. I mean after you were sort of Patient Zero with the Doctor Faust virus. I'm glad you cleared that up. It's weird how that virus metaphor kind of translates and people quarantined you like you were actually sick . . . that was so stupid. I tried to stay out of that. Language is so funny that way.

And here is his masterwork that the *Times* highlighted, called "College"—it's sort of hard to make out the graffiti if you aren't accustomed to it. It reads: "I diss doz in da past lookd down on my stuff."

So what are you up to? Oh? Really? Writing fiction? Ugh, I do not envy you! Fiction writing is a hard nut to crack. No no no, I TOTALLY think you should go ahead and write fiction! Look at the idiotic people getting in the *New Yorker* these days. It's an open field.

So are you filling out grants and stuff? (Huh, remember when you didn't fill out your Green Form? Was that you? That was beyond.) Mackakoon—it's the renowned artists' colony, right? Wow, best of luck—good luck with that. Not to crush your hopes, but—well, you know how difficult it is to get in there, right? It's sort of more for Emerging Artists and Writers—like on Tyler's level. But maybe if you try hard enough you can at least be in their Creative Helpers Food-Service program. It's the internship my nephew did. But don't get all depressed and mopey like you do if you get rejected. I think you get too discouraged too easily. You should keep trying! Art is so hard!

Oh, by the by, I got a Fuller Grant! Yeah! I'm going to Japan and Kazakhstan to study their rare magic rituals and create a Polaroid diary of the experience. It's weird I like wrote the grant on a total whim. Just one of those things. Do you know anything about folk rituals?

They're so fascinating. Oh that's right it was your major.

You should come to the celebration I'm having next week! Tyler will be there, and Sheila, who, in her spare time from being a successful businesswoman and lawyer just got the Lamont Younger Poets award. She's going to sing some of her poetry. And Tyler is going to show some of his crayon drawings of girl rock bands that were just bought by the MOMA.

And then Greta too. I guess you heard Greta's working on her second memoir. Did I tell you? Oh! Greta gotta Guggenheim! Greta gotta Guggie! Greta gotta Guggie! Yes! Fifteen thousand dollars! Which isn't so much but it's enough so that she can get a little studio so she can work on her photographs of stains. Amazing work.

And later in April here I'll be showing some of Carl's work. Just something he's doing on the side. Some of his Hate Poetry written on the back of Starbucks cozees. I supplied him with hundreds of them, because we get them at our annual Investor's Luau in Maui. If you miss it, you'll see it at the Whitney Biennial next fall.

You know, you should come by and leave flyers next time you have a show. We love to support the community here, and you can put your flyer, here, with all the other great things going on—teen spoken word and contact dance improv and a cappella groups. Feel free!

Now, my dear, if you'll excuse me, I'm going to mill about a bit. You have a great great night. Take care of yourself. Buh-bye.

The Mackakoon

C O L O N Y

Nestled in the hills of Upper Seachester, Mackakoon is one of America's most venerable literary institutions. For more than 150 years, the workshops, lectures, and classes held in the shadow of the Upper Region have provided a stimulating community of diverse voices in which we test our assumptions regarding art and literature. Thoreau, Hawthorne, Melville, Morrison, DeLillo, and Danticat have all made stops here.

The land was acquired in the nineteenth century by Mathias Milford, a breeder of Morgan horses, the proprietor of a local newspaper, and a spirited lover of nature. He added a cupola and three-story wings to the Victorian farmhouse on the property. Following his death, his daughter, the energetic spinster Millicent Milford, began to offer her house to poets and creators on their way to Boston. Miss Milford selflessly provided daily meals, light entertainment, quiet surroundings, and personal toilet attendance—an innovation at the time.

Millicent Milford *from an archival engraving*

To keep its creative charm alive, Mackakoon maintains a sense of authenticity. Every room has a fireplace (Honoreds and Fellows only). The milk is still unpasteurized and the rooms still have old-style water pails and chamber pots.

Mackakoon offers 3 kinds of residencies:

Honored Masters: Exalted teachers who lead workshops, like Toni Morrison, JT LeRoy, Charles Frazier, Jonathan Safran Foer.

Fellow Citizens: Those awarded entrance to Mackakoon may attend the weekly one-hour workshops and lectures.

Creative Helpers Food-Service:
Wait-listed applicants can attend Mackakoon in this effectively rewarding experience. These lively individuals, lovingly nicknamed "the Millicents," provide upkeep and a sense of rustic authenticity—maintaining the kitchen and completing light chore duties such as sweeping, hall-monitoring, and chamber pot disposal.

Application

Name _____

Address _____

Most recent book deal advance _____

What do you expect to accomplish at Mackakoon?

_____

What is H.D.'s full name? _____

Do you really really honestly consider yourself a writer?

_____

CASH _____ CHECK _____ CHARGE _____

Inner Odyssey

the Burning Man festival in Nevada's Black Rock Desert, 1999

Air My Breath, Water My Blood Earth My Flesh and Fire My Spirit . . .

All right now just the women sing, "Air My Breath, Water My Blood," and now the men "Earth My Flesh and Fire My Spirit . . ." Good! One more time—

Hello? Is that my friend? Well, hello. What a creative costume! Let me guess, you are supposed to be: a hedge-hog? A dust gnome? A sort of scarred, mutated survivor of the Apocalypse? That's not a costume? Right, the mud-flats. Yeah, it's pretty easy to lose your footing there.

Well you should dress up! It's half the fun of coming to Burning Man! Ten thousand people here for a week in the remote Nevada desert. A spontaneous community based on art and expression! We all are free to be whatever we want, following our innermost creative urges, who we really are in our souls.

Hm? Well thank you. Yes. I am a vulture of sorts. A bird at least. I am Perseus, God of Swiftness and Light. I know it's such a beautiful costume isn't it? So light and airy. It turns out that of all things I am best friends with Sally Rosenthal, the Academy Award-winning costume designer of my good friend Baz's last movie, and she just whipped this up for me, plus a few other changes for the course of the week. Fun, huh? I am so lucky.

Although I think this will be my last year here. I don't know it's kind of become overrun with lame partiers and desperadoes who don't really get the whole message. It's time for me to move on. Anyway, yay. You are here! How auspicious. Bless the Mother Moon! It really means a lot. You're someone I need to open my heart to more. This sacred place welcomes all, every type of person in every community, no matter what his or her level of success or means.

I just got back from the most beautiful Nudist Circle. Carl and Greta were there. They looked really good. Their bodies. You just missed them. We were celebrating their Letting.

Hm? Oh, yeah, you wouldn't understand that. I guess you would say that they "broke up," but that sounds so negative. They chose to finish their relationship, and celebrate its end, at the Nudist Circle. It was a beautiful ceremony. Lots of hands-on energy work. We all surrounded them, sang and coaxed the cords of their heart chakras to untangle. Yes, there were some tears, but Carl and Greta are still the best of friends. They just both knew that it was time. I'm so proud of them.

Hm? We didn't talk about you, actually. Wouldn't it be weird if, after all this time you thought Carl and you were going to, like, hook up again? Like . . . fifteen years after you dated? I know, so funny. Ha! But I am sure that is the last thing on your mind. You have so much going on now—your yoga, your sobriety. All that self-work.

Wait. How are you? Things are changing, huh? I can see it in your face, especially when I say "self-work." The anger, the frustration, the lines of concern in your forehead. Your face has changed from the pressure. It's not just aging, it's more of a shift in psyche. Hm.

Well it's good that you are here in the vast, open, healing Playa desert landscape. I really think it will do you some good. It's so grounding for people who have been too caught up in commercial consumerism and the petty, narrow goals it markets. Like "I have to have a rock band" or "I have to get into some fancy institution" and so forth. There isn't that "I need I need" vibe here, that vibe that lots of people have who have been overly toxified by our discouraging, spiritually contaminating "I need I need" culture. "I need someone to love me!" "I need to be successful!" "I need to have my old boyfriend pay attention to me when he doesn't!" It doesn't *matter* if you get those things, you know? I mean it's been nice for me to have those doors open, so I can let my light shine and give to my friends, but I would have been content without all of it, the money, the Fuller Grant, the fulfilling balanced relationships, the spiritually rewarding travels, everything. OK I know this is my spiel—but it's totally valid that less, you know, less experienced people may feel that "I need" pressure because it's just the way our culture works? But, here at the festival, it's more of a group thing. People just sort of . . . inspire each other . . .

It's funny I keep thinking of what Brad told me when I met him last summer on that archaeological dig in the Patagonia uplands. We had been working all day, just shoveling heavy clay in the hot sun with our shirts off, and he said, "You know, I have seen so much in my life: the movies, my beautiful wife, Jen, my ample free time to pursue my passion in architecture, being considered "Sexiest Man Alive" repeatedly by *People* magazine, but after all is said and done, it's times like these when I am beside other genuine souls, working on a common goal for mankind, that matter. Humanity is what I hold most dear." And then we walked down to Main Camp together. Silently. Feeling the humanity between us.

You know, I should introduce you to Grace Goodchild. She has this major system of self-discovery called The System that has really helped a lot of people. Basically you must ask yourself six questions: Are you really happy? Do you have a heart direction? What is your heart's story? What is your head's story? What is your story? What can you do with your story? She teaches people here to let their problems not affect them. How aging is actually caused through stress and stressful lifestyles. But whatever. I mean the way YOU handle stress is amazing. I mean you always somehow pull through don't you? You're like a hero with stress! Ha!

I can't believe that you are here! So . . . where's your water bottle?

You what? You don't have one?! No, actually it IS important. I mean you must have read the Burning Manual, right? That listed all the crucial items to bring? You didn't read it? You never GOT it?! Wow. OK, it's OK. Just start drinking now. Here, just start drinking from this jug.

Oooh. You hear that? It's the wind. Yeah. Looks like a major dust storm is coming. One of those hideous, evil dust storms that gets in your eyes and can blind you. So get your goggles ready.

You didn't bring those either? OH. Um . . . OK, no worries. Here . . . um, use this rag. That will kind of work. It'll be a challenge, but you'll be fine.

Where are you staying? Near the "Magic Caterpillar" tent? Oh those guys are so weird. But fun. Just don't have any of their mushroom stew! Ha ha!

You did? Well as long as you aren't on some radical personality pill like Zoloft or Askalar . . .

You—you are?

You STILL are?

—

You really got us in good this time, didn't you?

Hey, Talitha? Talitha? Could you, um, come here for a second? I'm going to need some help. My friend is going to be critically high in a matter of seconds.

Hello? Hello? OK, now just sit down right here. How many fingers am I holding up? Hello? OK, you'll be fine, you'll be fine. I know. No, of course I'm sure you're fine. No of course you can stand and see, but let's just sit down for a while, OK? Let's just sitty-sitty.

Hm? Hi Chloe! Oh my God I would love to go to the drum circle right now but this sort of friend of mine is freaking out a little. Just having a hard time. Yeah, first time. And also on Askalar. Yeah. Probably totally dehydrated too.

Do you want some tea? OK . . . let's get you some nice ginger tea. You're cool, you're cool . . . No I know you think you're fine . . . But we're just gonna sit here and breathe, OK?

Talitha, can you ask Jaweh to sound the community alert gong? And do you know where that neurologist from Berkeley is?

Oh wow. Do you see that far-off darkness? Do you hear that crackling? It's the dust storm. It's coming. Oh my God. This is a bad one. I've never seen the desert sky so angry. It's like a horizon of chewing locusts.

OK, breathe breathe. Feel the love I have for you. Drink some more water. Why don't you try repeating these words with me, OK? "Air my breath, Fire my spirit, Earth my body, Water my blood." And drink this water, lalala. No it's not blood you're drinking. It's water. It just looks like blood because it's just become dark out, dark as night. An enveloping darkness like a big black blanket. But it's definitely water. And you better drink it, blood or no blood, because it may be the last you'll have for a while. Wow you are really seeing things aren't you?

OK, calm down, breathe, breathe. You don't have goggles, so you better wrap this shirt tightly around your eyes. In the high wind of this storm, fine grains of sand will blow into them and pierce your corneas in a matter of seconds. So whatever you do, keep your eyes closed until I tell you to take off the blindfold . . . I mean, eye-shield. I know that with your hallucinatory state the last thing you want to do is keep your eyes closed because basically you now have to confront the visions that lurk in your subconscious, but unfortunately we don't have a choice here . . .

Phew! Do you hear that whistling? That sound, coming closer, coming closer. The land and air are merging into one. A screeching sky of demonic hawks. Does that seem what it looks like to you in your mind's eye?

No it's just that I remember seeing that from my own near-schizophrenic freak-out on mushrooms six years ago.

Does it seem like things are vibrating? Yeah. Things are going to start warping for you but I'm here, so let that be a comfort to you: I am here, and the world is real and I am your link to it, OK? So just remember we live in a consensual world. Remember we live in a consensual world.

Can you hear me? You probably can't. I probably sound far away. On the other end of a very long long tunnel. Like a voice pulling away, and peeling away everything solid and grounding with it. Until you are floating on a fabric made of detached whispers. A voice that slips inside your head, a secret you can barely keep. A haunt. A hate. Or maybe just the air.

Everyone hates you! No I didn't say that. I said hatred. I said haze. I said crazy you. I said I am so worried about you. No no no I don't mean to worry you. I'm just worried about you. Do you hear me? Do you, do you? Do you do? Hell? Hell? Hello?

You're coughing! Are you OK? Are you OK? Hokay? Hacking? You're hacking. The dust is in your lungs. Ooh. How do you feel? You may feel the wind blowing and reaching inside you, don't you? You may feel the dust in a breath that travels to your feet. That dust, full of the smallest particles, little needleheads, that may lodge in your skin and through your throat and down into your intestines. That dust is so pervasive. Made of so much filth. Yuck. I hate the dust, don't you? It's been everywhere. The same dust that coats the tops of televisions, that gums up the axle oil of SUVs. That chokes out smoke from poultry farms and pesticide plants. Dust made of crusts in hungry Third World eyes, the little flecks of pollen on dirty flies, the dust that's made of ground bones from old mass graves and bacterial spores from seeping landfills piled with our ignorant waste. But the dust is good too, no it's good, it's good. Good dust, good dust. Dust mingling among your old toys in your parents' basement and the put-away porcelain figurines of your dead grandparents, the dust that's accruing on the acid-free paper of your "I'm-so-lonely" diaries, and letters to friends you've forgotten. Dust hovering in the libraries. Flecks from the etchings in ancient stones, fibers of Egyptian papyrus, the expectorated graphite from the drafts of constitutions. All the knowledge ever known, blowing. This accordion of chronology we exist in. A mist of hissing history. You're alone in the blowing known. Just the dust. Flitting like careless androgynous dancers in circles and circles. Consensual concentric circles. Consexual consensual circles. Bones and ashes and dust. The dust is around you. The androgynous dancers are dodging you. It's a dungeon of dust. Exogenous exoskeletons. Existential concerns. Spews and spews. Where are you? Where am I? I'm who? You? No

I'm you, not me, you. You knew. Spews and spews. Do you?

Wait don't run away! You'll get lost! Maybe fatally! I can't see where you are! The dust is so thick! This is bad! I can't see you! Where are you call my name! I am here! Follow my voice through the darkness! Oh my God this is terrible. Reach through the cloud you cackling crazy! You're cackling calm down! Calm down, calm down.

Close your eyes breathe into the rag. Maybe calm yourself by asking some questions. Curiosity is a life-force. It's soothing. It keeps us going. Ask into the wind, its howling, speckled mouth. Are you cold? What day is it? What did you have to eat this morning? What's your name? Who are you? Are you really happy? Do you have a heart direction? Do you have a head direction? What is your heart's story? How common is breakage? Will you be able to return the product if it is broken? How can you tell if a trend is too young for you? Is there a counselor or clergyman you could talk to? What if you tried to like someone you weren't attracted to and felt just as unsatisfied? Are you ready for a new sensation? Is it normal to need more care? What is your head's story? Do you do too much work? Are you fooling yourself? Does anyone love you? Did you miss your chance? Have you lost your bloom? How do you feel when you're alone in your bedroom? Are you your real self on Askalar?

You may feel like all the dust is flying into your lungs. In case you were wondering, here's what's happening to you medically: the decrease in oxygen makes the lungs want to shunt. Your body gives itself an emergency cardiovascular reevaluation and when the units per O_2 content reach five point one milliliter per minute and the number of plasma is 102, the salutatory function shuts down. This renders the respiratory zone of the lung essentially inactive: vein bronchials, mucus cells, and terminal bronchial cells are deadened and your skin begins to dry kind of like a scab, peeling away layer by layer and the wet undersides scabbing and flaking away until you have lost at least an inch of skin before losing consciousness. You may have survived if you had that one small extra tablespoon of liquid in your system, but that one small bit of water is gone. Sucked away. By Askalar. Yes, Askalar. You probably never drank the seven eight-ounce glasses of water as prescribed, did you? Ask yourself that. Ask. Ask. Askalar.

It's easy, death. It's a breeze. It's getting closer. Whispering and asking.

Listen.

Life After Death

face down in the dirt of the desert, next morning, 1999

Hello . . . sweetie, wake up . . . wakey wakey . . .

Oh! Hold on, no stop swatting at the air! Your lungs are not turning into dust, no no. There are no voices. What are you going on about? It's daytime . . . put your hands down . . .

Oh sweetie, you're raving. I told you it would be an intense trip. Shh. You'll wake up half the camp. Just relax. Just be in reality, clarity. I'm not saying anything about any weird evil dust. No you aren't lost in some cloud. Satanic television snow? There is no void swallowing you. What does that mean? What are you talking about? You're raving. You're so funny, little crazy one. Shh, shh. The worst of it is over. Well, almost.

Oh wow that is a big bruise! Jeez did you fall on your ass that hard?

Oh. That's your Kermit the Frog tattoo. I guess it's gotten a little blurry and stretched out as you've gotten older.

Oooh. Yeah. You feel crampy, huh? Yeah, it's the toxins trying to release from your body. Those mushrooms from the Caterpillar tent, mixed with the harsh chemicals of Askalar basically turn into a big box of Ex-Lax after eight hours. Yeah, you'll be shittin' like there's no tomorrow in a sec. I just need to make sure you don't expel blood or your liver or whatever. The convulsions can get pretty strong. But the open air is good for your system, which is about to experience some serious uncontrollable digestive seizures.

Talitha? It's time. Gather everyone for the healing circle.

Burning Man-ual Things to bring

* Goggles & Dust Masks — (don't leave home without 'em)
* Tent (buy a cheap one — anything you take out there will get ruined)
* Warm Sleeping Bag! (and Extra Blankets?) and pillow(s)
* Lantern (only tinted or tucturnal filaments, please)
* Duct tape, bungee cords, cable ties, work gloves (why ask why?)
* Tribal Art — Sculptures, Totems, Flags, Banners
* Water! — bring at least a gallon per person per day (I drink more)
* Gatorade or some other rehydrating drink
* Snack bars, trail mix, dried fruit, jerky, peanut butter
* Spare toilet paper (buy the porta-potty-safe stuff — usually available in RV shops)
* Self Esteem — be sure you leave feelings of low self-worth at home. They have a tendency to severely dehydrate you
* Sunblock + Aloe for post-burn
* Foot care (lotions, salts, mole-skin)
* 2 Pocket-sized generators
* make-up (body paints, glitter gels)
* Tampons, Condoms, Prescription meds, etc. (be sure to read warning labels!)
* and, most importantly, bring **An Open Heart** and the **Ability to Forgive Your Enemies**

Loyal Companions

catching up at the dog run, 2000

Breaker! Breaker! Here, boy! Aw good dog Breaker! You are the best dog in the world. Yes you are! Yes you are!

Hi! Oh my God, someone was just talking about you! You look so sporty! Did get your hair straightened or just not wash it for a while?

Aw, and look there's little Checkers! Wow. How is Checkers?

Oh. I'm sorry to hear that. But yeah, I can tell. He seems so low-energy. Like his little dog soul is tired, ready to pass on into dog heaven. It's just a matter of time, you know, since you got Checkers at that pet shop, which was so gracious of you, to take in an animal that is sure to be stunted and a little disadvantaged because basically the pet shop industry is another form of animal cruelty. Dog diseases can be so cruel.

Breeding is just so important. It just gives dogs the life skills they need to survive and handle stress. There are dogs that somehow have the training in their blood to react to life like warriors, like hunters. And then there are dogs who may have never been designed to survive. Who, if the world were more natural, would be slaughtered in the wild like wildebeests. Victim dogs.

Anyway. Are you OK . . . now? You know, after all that weirdness you went through? It's just I remember last time I saw you, you were, you know . . . a little mentally compromised. It was kind of harsh. You really lashed out at me. But I know you didn't mean it, since I basically saved your life. I really, really hope things are better for you now.

Breaker! Breaker! Get out of that bush!

Oh hi Drew! How are you? How was your trip? Breaker is great. Aw and there's Flossie! Look at the two of them going at it! Ha ha, always so frisky. They are so in love! Listen I would be happy to take care of Flossie next time you go away on a shoot, OK?

Breaker and Drew's dog Flossie are so in love. Animals are just so open to love. So healthy and honest about their feelings. With the right upbringing. Sigh. Love is really what it's about, isn't it, in the end?

Which is why shows like *Sex and the City* are so popular I suppose. Have you been watching it? You don't? I actually sort of like it. You think she's dumb, right? Yeah it's funny, Sarah Jess is actually really cool. She's actually really generous with her friends, Ess Jess. Hum.

No I'm not laughing at you, I just think it's funny how some people react when someone is more successful than them? I'm not saying you are doing it, I just think it's funny. But I have to say, I don't know how you do it. I am *so glad* I am not single. It looks so hard. I mean, look at you! You're so tired all the time from going out! It's unfair. For someone so nice and standard as you.

No wait you are? You are dating someone! That's great! "The End of the Dry Spell"! Who are you seeing now? Lyle? Lyle who? No, tell me. I may know him.

Lyle FRANKLIN? LYLE? Oh my God Lyle! He is single again? No, I just thought he was seeing someone. He's single? That is great that he is trying to focus again, I mean maybe this time it'll work. Wow, Lyle Franklin is single. "The Bisexual Bachelor."

He didn't tell you? He's so funny. Well, don't stress over it. I mean that would really freak him out if he saw you stressing over him, you know? Ha! That's the worst thing you could do is stress over it.

I always forget. Is it you or my friend Andrea who breaks out in bad acne when you get stressed?

Breaker, come now, back away from that female poodle.

Breaker is such a flirt. Especially with his big you-know-what. You can imagine what a Casanova he is in the dog run.

And . . . when I'm not busy keeping Breaker in line (Ha! Ha!) I've been, you know doin' my stuff . . . Me? I've been good. Well actually better than good. I mean, so much so that it's kind of scary. You know everyone's been talking about how hard the economy has been for them? Frankly, I am finding it cleansing. It's just a time for me to really focus on what I really want to do, instead of those flush '90s years when I was so busy buying key property and launching my handbag business. I mean I can't complain about the big bucks I made, but I think I am finally doing what I love. It's so fulfilling to work ten hours a day doing something that you love, you know? And of course I just saved tons of money. Now I have the time for focusing on my art, taking up the guitar again, seeing old Silicon Alley pals . . .

Here, Breaker, play with your dried hog bone! Play with your dried hog bone! Good boy Breaker!

And it's sort of going pretty well. I mean it's one of those things where you visualize your dreams and they can happen, even in these uncertain times. It all started coming together for me last fall. Oh, at that party I saw you at. Remember how you were tired and went home early? Well it ended up being a crazy night! I ran into my friend on the street who was on her way to Ess Jess and Matthew's party for Mos Def. It was just a little party, at their house. I got talked into going, even though I was so tired (like you were!) and ready to just go home and finish my Whitney Studio Program application (I got in!) and I flopped down on the couch next to Edie Falco of all people. Of course I totally had to suppress gushing to her how about much I respect her work as an actress and how I have loved her even from her beginning days as a stage actress Off Broadway. We were talking about how she's really worried that there are no roles for older women.

"Don't you have a boyfriend?" she asked.

I said "Yes, but I'm unusual that way, especially in this city."

And she just got really honest and said "I'm going to end up alone, but it's fine since I'm financially independent." It was just so funny. I thought of you because I know how much you want that financial part. It was just so funny. She's just so cool. Anyway we all ended up playing this extremely fun French improv parlor game, where you have to write down a story and people act it out. Mos and I did this hilarious but very political scene written by this amazing woman Suzan, who has the hottest play on Broadway right now. It was a short hip-hop interpretation of the Koran. Very controversial.

The next day I got a call from Suzan who wanted to meet up with me and "discuss my work." I don't know, but we met up and I guess she liked my parlor game performance and thinks that I should be in her next incredibly incendiary play in the fall. So.

It's almost not surprising. I mean I don't mean to sound arrogant. It's just that I went to this amazing, amazing psychic the other day. She told me the most amazing stuff about how I have a special connection with the sun.

Breaker! Leave Checkers alone! Don't tease poor little Checkers!

You know how the sun is really an exploded star and how lately there have been reports that it is flaring uncontrollably? How the Apocalypse is just around the corner? Well I am one of the few people who benefit from this situation. Astrologically. It's weird. I'm apparently getting stronger and reaching my goals, and have—oh! This is weird, but YOU came up. I was so surprised. But she told me to tell you "not to drink and drive"? And also that you should watch out for "the man who seems like he likes you"? Do you know what that may mean? Weird, huh?

Her house was amazing—full of ancient artifacts and cultural symbols from her many travels. She showed me these Guatemalan dolls she keeps in a tiny little pillbox. They are called the Worry People. She took them out and sprinkled them in her hand. There was a little baby and a mother and a bus driver and an old woman and a few others. Tiny little things. Apparently they speak to her and tell her things about the Other Side. They were the ones who told me I would get into the Whitney. They also gossip about each other—especially the old woman. God . . . could you imagine being stuck in a box with the same group of people and never escaping them?—and, even worse, someone gossiping about you for eternity? Scary!

Breaker! Be kind to Checkers! Let him hump your leg . . . he's dying. He just wants some love. Let poor little gay, dying Checkers hump your leg.

It must be so hard to have the one thing that loves you unconditionally begin to pass from this world. I thought I was never going to love again after Nicky died, but I survived.

It's just that I have been through SO MUCH the past few years. I really feel like I have paid my dues, you know? I'm always helping everyone. And now I just want to be successful so I can give more to candidates I believe in, artists I believe in like Tyler, theatrical efforts I believe in like Sam's new play, businesses that I feel are bettering the planet, and people who just need a boost like Greta and Carl. And, like, help you from getting permanent brain damage in the desert.

And Sheila's amazing new business! Oh God, remember Sheila? Oh. Of course you know her. I just forgot, because she had a hard time remembering you the other day. I just saw her at a little small get-together at Sam's. We were all having a small party for Jacob for his new album, just a circle of close friends together showing support. It was secretly to thank Sheila for getting Jacob's career rolling so long ago.

Oh! Remember how Sheila wanted us to invest in her dumb idea—you know, some rack that would hold postcards? I know you said it sounded like a scam. Ya big cynic! Well she was laughing about that because that "scam" now happens to be those MAX RACKS that are EVERYWHERE! You know, those postcard racks that are in like every bar and restaurant? Hello! Now she's richer than Barry Diller or whatever. And, actually when your name came up the other day, she remembered you eventually and how you called it a scam and she laughed about it. She uses that story as part of a motivational speech she gives to mentally frustrated people, about how you should never be discouraged no matter what people say. Anyway, she said to say "hi" to you. I told her about your little . . . your times . . . your projects.

Greta was there. Single again, looking GREAT. It's weird she just sort of bounced off of being so in a couple to being single without a problem really. I mean you and Carl were so much younger when you broke up so it was a different thing. More affecting.

Isn't that right, Breaker? You are the hottest dog in the world. Yes you are! The most gorgeous, hottest, Top Model–looks dog in the whole wide world, yes you are! Yes you are!

So how's the job hunt? Ugh, what a difficult time to find work, much less do something fulfilling. Please let me know if I can do anything, 'kay? Actually, my friend Adam is writing an extensive article for the *New Yorker* about all that. He's calling it "Generation Jobless." You should get in touch with him. Maybe it would be good to articulate how you are feeling.

I will totally keep an eye out for you, though. Have you ever thought about being an assistant for museum security? Or a cater-waiter? That may be something for you to look into. I hear since the smoking ban, a lot of people are making money by selling single cigarettes on the street in front of bars. I'm not saying you should do that, I just meant that there are opportunities right under your nose. You never know. Anyway, good luck!

Breaker! Breaker! Here, boy! We have to go! Time for our two-hour uphill power hike and then Doggie Yoga!

See you soon, OK?

Desirable
Aquirables

This bag's rare vitello leather comes from Poland where young farm-raised calves roam in open pastures, leaving their skin with few markings, free of the scarring from barbed wire seen in harsher industrial ranching. These smooth-skinned animals are gently killed in their youth, and their bodies are sent to Kraków, where trained Skin Butchers cut away to the softest underbelly of the animal (the rest is thrown away). The skins are brought to a town near Palazzo, Italy, where tanners use a special medieval technique, treating them with natural vegetable dye that keeps the pores open to allow the rare, soft baby calfskin to breathe. Then, at a small factory outside of Abano, the buttery pelts are hammered entirely by hand (no prefab bits or outsourced pieces) into this luxurious, opulent bag.

$^\$$**1950**, buylust.com *for store info.*

In the Real World

a run-in at the *ShopShape* magazine launch party sponsored by Señor Strawberry Liqueur, early 2001

Oh hey! I haven't seen you in a long time! So . . . what are you here for? Oh. You're catering? Oh I see. That's why you are wearing a huge sombrero and kooky little poncho. It's a promotional thing for Señor Strawberry Liqueur. I thought that was, like, your whole "going somewhere fancy" outfit. I'm so dumb! Wow well tell your boss she did an amazing job designing this party! It looks so fun! Really fun! The castanets are a nice touch.

Oh, no no. I don't touch harsh alcohol. But, um, so long as you're offering, could I have another Amstel Carbless? Can I just rest my bottle on your tray?

Wait a second. Did I see you more recently? Like on TV or something?? Like were you one of the wacky competitors on that reality show, *Who Da Fool?*

Yes! I was right that WAS you! It's so cool that you did that . . . what season of *Who Da Fool?* was it again? *Who*

Da Fool 4? 5? 16–17 million! Ha ha. That's GREAT. No! Really! It's very very very cool. Especially to put a face on people who suffer from sexual side effects from Askalar . . . just to show that there are NORMAL people in the world with Disorder who are coping.

Wow those ads for the show are so omnipresent. Good for you! Good for you! Did you pick out your own clothes for the show? Wow have you blown up! I mean on TV!

So now you are here.

Yeah . . . I guess those reality shows really don't result in much money, do they? That's the great myth of them, isn't it? It's so easy to get drawn in. Like Emmanuel Lewis, or some other child television actor so warped by his own fame that it stunts his growth, and he eventually ends up a punch line. Funny, our world.

It's so weird, I was watching TV, sort of half asleep after a long day and three-hour strenuous Pookalan workout and I kind of half recognized you but kind of didn't? And I just was sort of vaguely paying attention and said to myself—who are those jackasses on TV? And then you came on! But you look really tan and golden—did they touch you up a lot with all their weird caked TV makeup?

Wow, you had to build a fort, and eat that horse bladder and create a small oven. That is really cool. Too bad you didn't win. But I'm sure that it will lead to something. Who was that reality show "survivor" last season who appeared in *Teen Playboy*? I can't remember her name. Well I am sure it will lead to something.

Oh wait I'm getting a text message from my boyfriend Viggo. Huh. Hee hee! Aw, how cute. Sorry. I just got distracted for a sec.

So, were you hired by a catering company or directly by *ShopShape* magazine? Uh huh. Uh huh. It's amazing the success of that magazine! How it's utterly transformed the industry. I'm so proud of Karen, the Editor in Chief, who is weirdly a close friend of mine from Collage class at Parsons. She helped me with my business plan for my handbag line that I had, which I loved but sold the rights to just because I wanted to do more creative work. But I still have a consulting position in the company.

Me, me, me. What am I saying. What about you. I mean it's so weird I was just thinking about you because I was listening to No Doubt. Wow their new album reminds me so much of your '90s coffeehouse band. It's weird how similar you sound! Did you ever copyright any of that stuff? No? Too bad. I was going to tell you to do that at the time but I didn't know if you'd really motivate to do it.

Holy crap, I didn't know you were still playing music! That's amazing that you have stuck with it so long, through all the changes and trends and styles and aging. I mean, the general audience for that kind of stuff is preteens—and you're a thirty-four-year-old! You're you! It's just very cool that you're taking that commercial and financial risk, and trying to bridge generations.

Me? I'm fine I'm fine . . . you know, working with Robert Wilson and Tom Waits on their next world-touring experimental staged opera . . .

You didn't know? Oh. I guess I've been sort of mellow and unpromotional about it. I more let people ask me. They just liked my compositions and we have been working on a four-part retelling of Cherokee legends. You know those guys, always trying to do something that will be timeless and sustaining, yadda yadda. They are so funny. They have worked together for so long now that they finish each other's sentences.

I don't know how I hooked up with them really. I just thought to myself: "I am in my thirties now and I need to sort of evolve and do grown-up work." You know? And it was one of those things where you think it and then you ARE it? Because that next week my boyfriend Viggo introduced me to Bobby and Tommy and the next thing I knew I was in rehearsals five nights a week. So there you go! We've both been so busy!

Oh, pardon me for one second.

Hi Michelle! I know I'm so tired today too!

Wow doesn't she look haggard and tired. She's working here at *ManMade*, the men's version of *ShopShape*. Wow, she really looks like she's been through something! Offices are so toxic!

Actually I wish I had seen you about a year ago because I was at South by Southwest, and weirdly became good, good friends with that incredibly well-known music producer, Danny Lanois. I needed a place to stay and he said, "Why don't you just stay with me up at Lucinda Williams's house?" And of course I had to suppress my complete giddy shock that I was going to stay at her house—I mean, Lucinda Williams is like a living icon of Alt-Country Rock! So I did and we had a great time just drinkin' Pabst and shooting tin cans and stuff. She is really as cool as she seems. I helped her with her lyrics on her new, widely praised album. Anyway I was thinking about you because it's the kind of thing you used to say you would, like, slit your face off to do just once.

You. Um. You're kind of . . . um. You're in someone's way. Behind you.

Sorry sir . . .

Do you . . . need to pass around those spinach quiches? I can wait here if you need to, like, do some work or something.

Did you get Jacob's new album? I mean how could you not. He's like the Garth Brooks of modern rock. Or like the alive Kurt Cobain without the fatal depression. He's so cute. He really charmed the A&R reps because he sent out cassette tapes instead of spending all that money on the latest technology. People found it endearing and kind of raw and real. It gives his music a warmer sound. You think he's sold out? I think his album *The Education of Jacob* is actually great.

No I totally, totally understand your point. I totally do. Sure sure sure. It just bums me out how some people are stuck on the idea that just because somebody makes money they aren't talented. It's sort of like what you tried to do with Sheila. Which is fine if you want to speak out but it smells sour, you know? I'm not saying that that is what you are arguing! I just think there's some smell to it. To that general argument. The general argument smells sour.

Are they vegemarian? The quiches. They are? OK if you don't mind I would love one.

Meanwhile remember Frank Spitz? From college? He was a TA for that lame Folk and Myth seminar—that one I withdrew from? I think you wanted openly to have sex with him?

Anyway, well it ends up that he and his beautiful former student–wife settled down happily in Clarkwellsville and have this beautiful daughter now, Boo, who is eleven (can you believe it? We're so old! Hahaha!) and was just signed to Arista. Apparently she is so musical and she composed an entire cycle of songs on her little Sponge-Bob SquarePants Blackberry Beeper. Kids these days! It's almost like we cynical Generation Xers should just hang it up and let Gen Next bulldoze over culture with their talent and uncomplicated facility in the marketplace. See? You really paved the way!

And guess who is directing the video. Yup, me. I know—crazy. It's a really empowering song of female pride, called "Eat My Pink Pudding."

Oh—I think your catering coordinator is waving for you to come over there. I hope he's not mad at you. Sorry. This is so weird but could you bring me another Amstel Carbless? I'm feeling a little hot suddenly. Do I look red? Like around the edge of my jawline? It feels so hot in here. Shit. Wait.

Listen, do these spinach quiches have any meat in them? They don't? Are you sure? Not any oils? Are you sure they are vegemarian? Vegemarian, not vegetarian! No, I'm sorry but there IS a big difference! Vegemarian means that they have been prepared on separate preparation areas than meat products! You know I have been strictly vegemarian for twelve years and if I have any meat oils or essences even near me I will suffer a radical allergic attack! Haw! Huh! Breathe, goff!

Please go get me a glass of unsparkling water with lemon!

LIL' BOO - ATLANTIC RECORDS
MUSIC VIDEO NARRATIVE TREATMENT
BY U.

EAT MY PINK PUDDING

Already the hottest record on the radio, in the clubs, and out on the streets, this record can only go one more place – through the roof. This is a night no one will ever forget.

In this clip, we will establish Lil' Boo as the Princess of Hip Pop. Imagine a legendary party spot from the old days revamped to reflect the new times...raw-edged, slightly grimy with exposed pipes, air ducts, fixtures...but with a flair and unique allure. This is a place where the glitter meets the gutter, and tonight it's packed.

We open to a nighttime exterior shot of Lil' Boo with her people, leaning on a row of shiny high-end cars and trucks – Jags, Escalades, Benzes, Hummers, etc. Boo is next to a "pimped-out" 2003 BMW 745. Even with a full Cavalli mink on, we're already drooling.

Around her is a thugged-out band, dressed in black, with platinum horns and other instruments. This is no high school marching band, but a collection of gangsta types that keep the crowd jumping. Timbaland could star as the bandleader.

Inside the club, there's a diverse party crowd with beautiful women and thugs, all waiting for the show to start. The anticipation is so thick it's sweating off the ceiling. When Boo hits the stage, it's like a fuse has just been lit and, in a hail of lights and hands in the air, the crowd explodes... As she plunges into "Pink Pudding," a sea of bodies pulsate in one collective rhythm all around her. Boo will look exquisite as she works the stage, always lit and framed in tight angles that showcase her talents and highlight her hot sexy 11-year-old beauty.

Wartime

spotted at Kinko's, late 2001

Hey! It's genuinely so good to see you!

No, really. I know a lot of people seem so false when they say that to you, but I mean it. I just have been through so much lately I appreciate even the smallest contact with my friends. Or anyone, really. And everything seems so small now, in comparison to the . . . you know the . . . the Crisis. All those petty differences don't matter. Like I totally don't even care anymore that you served me food I was allergic to and I almost died, you know? All that stuff just doesn't matter.

What are you here for? Photocopying your résumé. On mid-weight paper. Wow, fancy fancy. Well good luck. The job market has really suffered, hasn't it?

So what have you been doing? How are you? Getting by? Kind of watching the war and world events on CNN in shock? Yeah . . .

Well I wasn't really that surprised because I'd read the Hart-Rudman report, and I met Condi through Sheila at a small dinner. So I sort of knew about how things were getting serious. So, but—I just couldn't sit by and be all inactive. And then weirdly my friend Bertrand, who is a French photojournalist, called me. I picked up the phone and without saying hello he said, "How would you like to make a difference?" Yeah, I know it sounds weird, but it isn't weird if you know him and our relationship. He's just more . . . more . . . direct and honest than a lot of people in this country?

I mean I know that you probably read up on everything that's happening . . . like in *Time,* and the *New York Times,* and the *Nation* or whatever. To be honest I try to get a more balanced view. These days I get most of my news from BBC World and aljazeera.net.

Anyway Bertrand knew of my capabilities and magic ability to pick up languages and asked me to accompany him as an embedded reporter for NBC. They call it the "Pulitzer Package" because you kind of always end up with one, but it's sort of an inside joke among top journalists.

Damn, the lights are bright in here. Do you have a tan? No? Oh, it just looks like you have a tan.

Anyways, I was unwittingly dragged into this underworld and shown things about Afghanistan and the lives of Afghans that few people have seen before. So. All my notes are being translated (I sometimes write in Arabic) into a new book! It's weird when you are one of a handful of people in our culture to experience what Bertrand calls "The Other Side of the Paradigm." To think people were here just reading *Vanity Fair* and everything went on just as superficially because no one had the courage to make a difference.

Oh wow I see you're putting your résumé on blue paper, with a Helvetica font! Wow, how nontraditional. Personally I would go for something more readable and conservative like a clean Times Roman font, but that's just me. You are always pushing the envelope, so to speak. And it's great. People need to see that kind of résumé every now and then.

Are you printing from here? Ooh. I hope you have a firewall on your computer. Or basically you are a raw, red open wound for all sorts of computer viruses. This place is like a public rest room of worms and computer bacteria. And I SERIOUSLY hope you backed everything up!

So I'm just here getting my manuscript copied for backup, because the original is going to Vassar—they're acquiring my old manuscripts and those Polaroids I took on the Fuller. I said I'd Xerox it myself because I don't like special favors. Like I still ride the subway.

And whatever about the Pulitzer. I'd really rather not think about it. It's weird how tan you look. Did you go to like a tanning salon? No?

Sooo, anyway. Are you traveling at all? You went to Boston, good for you! And you are going to Miami! That's OK! Did you get a cool place? Right. Right. Good old simple easy Miami. Sigh. I miss those simpler days of mine. I just worry about you there, since so many people don't really go there anymore.

Oh wait. I get it. Did you put on a lot of self-tanner? Is that why your color is so different? No, it looks good. It's a little speckled on your face but in a natural way.

Have you seen Sebastian here yet? I was supposed to meet him. Sebastian? You know, the celebrated adventurer-author with burning blue eyes and a hot naturally toned body. I met him in Jalalabad with Bertrand and Bikna. Bikna was my translator. She is a self-sacrificing Afghani woman and she brought me through Kabul. She was such a beautiful, humble, truthful woman. She wears cotton and rough silk, and sometimes a headscarf.

Every day was a challenge. And there is nothing like the real, true feeling that you are surviving every minute to really bring life into focus. You may have gotten a kind of simulated taste of this feeling from your stint on *Who Da Fool?* when you had sex with the gym teacher from New Jersey.

But it's sort of the exact opposite of that drunken club life here. Which is so hard on sexualizing young girls, who are just getting their strength when they're totally taken advantage of. Speaking of, are you still dating that DJ/ Gossip Columnist and just sort of keeping it light like he wanted to? How fun! That is so cute. What a cute couple I bet you are. I am so psyched for you! Do you think it's actually going to go somewhere this time?

Speaking of Hollywood. Hey. Guess what. I wrote my first full-length screenplay! Its called *Devil's Dogs*. I'm here copying that too. Yes, let it be known! Ha! With so much pain in the world it's so good to know I have that, you know?

Well, it's sort of amazing how it happened. I think it was perhaps the night that I was helping some young Afghani children to safety from a bombing in their township that I fell in love with screenwriting. I ran into the Doctors Without Borders hospital, and guess who was there but Sebastian, who was just on an exploratory tour, but also volunteering with local refugee camps. In our spare time he gave me a concentrated, rigorous short writing Master Class.

We spent some time with him, but then Bertrand and I went on through the countryside. He and I just shared our energy and spoke about how there is such hardship here and what we wanted to express to the people back in our countries. And we whipped up a whole outline of *Devil's Dogs*. We went hiking to a beach in a beautiful part of the country that our confining propagandistic media would never show of Afghanistan. Bikna made us some traditional *pashjabi* and we ate it in our tent, looking up at the stars. Then she lit some small gas lanterns around our tent, casting a beautiful red romantic glow. And we slept up there. For a few days . . .

OK, well now you know, and for obvious reasons it's just really really important that you don't tell anyone. I mean pretty much everyone I have told is in the industry, so they sort of inherently know that huge huge photojournalists like Bertrand need to keep their personal lives completely quiet. So if it leaks to the *Star* or anywhere that we're dating then we'll know you leaked it!

Just jokin', no big whoop. But, you know, at the same time. Keep it on the DL, OK?

Look, your résumé is ready. Wow. It looks great! That font is so eye-catching. It really wakes up the eye! It will definitely grab the attention of the interns and office assistants who open up the mail and sort the hundreds and hundreds of submissions that businesses are receiving these days when they post job openings. Oh, wait, um. I don't know if this matters to you, but in your address? It looks like your street name isn't capitalized. I mean it's totally minor but it's one of those details that could put you straight in the "No" pile. Ugh, I hate niggling things like that! That's another fifty buckaroos to recopy! Bummer! You should ask me to proofread next time!

Oh what great timing, my manuscript is ready.

Could you just put that on my CAA account? Thanks so much.

So I leave you now, my dear. You be good to yourself, you hear me? Bye.

FOR YOUR CONSIDERATION

Sam Fuller

in

Devil's Dogs

War is Hell.
But for the Devils, it's *Home*.

Sam Fuller for Best Lead Actor in a Drama
Elayna Pierce for Best Supporting Actress
Best Original Screenplay

Office Job

in the cafeteria of the Condé Nast building, 2003

Oh. My. God. Now this is a sight I thought I would never see. The last dilettante of Clarkwell College . . . of AMERICA, with a full-time job! I mean I know you have worked all your adult life but this seems significant. Wow you actually look good all tucked in and officey. Well congratulations. Welcome to the real world. I guess your credit card debt caught up to ya, huh? Ha ha.

Do you know what's in the international food line? I hope its Antillean chicken again. I just want some simple greens and a small spiced chicken breast. That's all I really need. So what's on the menu? You don't know? But I thought you worked here.

OH oh oh oh. I am so spaced out. I thought you said you worked HERE—like you were the new buffet line attendant. You work at a magazine?

Wowee, you have come a long way. A LONG way. Congratulations! It makes so much sense because you seemed sort of low energy at Kinko's. People with nine to five jobs have all this built-up negativity from working all week and then it's so hard to enjoy yourself on the weekend, right?

Ha ha, I was just thinking about you today. About how we used to laugh about that Burning Man trip. That Burning Man trip, remember? Wow you were trashed. The pictures of you are *chilling*. And there was that dust storm . . . hahahaha. I was rushing around like crazy making sure you were hydrated, saving your life, hahahaha.

Wait! Stay and talk! Tell me your news!

Where are you working? *Kids' Vogue*? How great. Wow. I thought that was being discontinued. No, sorry. I just heard. Well no worries. Once you get in this building you pretty much never leave, so I am sure that you can roll over to some position of equal or lesser stature at another book.

You know, I am so sorry I haven't been in touch. I have been really really busy. Not even enough time for myself even. Just running around! "Hey photograph this!"

"Hey curate this!" "Hey will you be the spokesperson for our premium jeans line!" Go away, you know? Not enough time for myself even.

And I miss you! We should really be more in touch. I hate how we drifted apart. Ha! Sheila and I were laughing so much about that story you told us. How you lost your virginity at Pi Kap to a guy wearing a mud mask for blackheads? That should definitely go into some routine of yours. Or profile or skit. You are still writing, right? And trying to do what you do? Well, the mud mask story is so funny! It should at least go in your "itogether" profile.

No, yeah, no I know you are on it. Yes of course it's anonymous, but Sheila told me. Well along with the Max Rax, she owns "itogether.com." Personally I think it's cool! It's cool that you are on the market and over the typical dumb age on those sites! It's really the way to go for singles over thirty-five. And you seem like you haven't had micro and Botox and all that junk, so you look like a regular person with a regular complexion, so that's even better.

Oh my God before I forget, she told me to tell you that your DESPERATE DATER™ profile with the subject line "I'm really really lonely" is down. I guess the system can't like have up entries that have low response . . . something about it blocking the flow of the system.

No! Don't be embarrassed! There's nothing wrong with Internet dating! It's just good practice for people who haven't learned how to talk like normal in normal situations. A good training ground! And anyway you look sexy the way your body looks now. You're not too fat.

You're eating bread pudding? How brave. It's like the embodiment of carbs.

But I gotta get a move on because I am up to my goiter in work! I'm just directing one of Jacob's new videos. Have you heard it? His new single, "The Lost One," is going to be huge.

Hm? Oh yeah, no no no no. I don't work here. God I don't know how you can handle it. I could never do the nine to five thing. (More like nine to eight, right? Ha ha!) Everyone is so well dressed and there is such high pressure. Ulcer City!

I'm here for a photo shoot for *Vanity Fair*. Another year-end wrap-up feature from the prominent portraitist of our time, Annie Liebowitz. This year I think Leo is "The Raconteur," Dame Judi Dench is "The Maven," and I guess I am "The Virtuoso" or something like that. She's taking my picture in front of some burning oil cans and '90s bric-a-brac. Very real, rough, recession-y. I think just to show how I am a survivor, and come from humble beginnings and all that. You know how magazines are. They love that kind of stuff.

You do seem stressed though. But good-stressed. Stress doesn't always have to be bad, you know? Stress is sometimes good for getting work done. And I read in *Simple Organic Makeovers* magazine that it actually can boost your immune system.

You know, why don't you call me? I would love to have you over to my waterfront property. It's so relaxing there, and I have this great tea garden that Tyler designed, and Carl constructed this cute veranda for me out of recyclable plastic liter bottles.

It's just sometimes when your life is going really well and you are peaking with ambition like you are now, you kind of forget to find time for yourself and your friends. You forget the more important things in life. Like close friendships and relationships. I read that in *Simple Organic Makeovers* too. Just keep that in mind, you know? You know how headfirst you are.

You don't remember my cell number? Well here it is again. You never know when you'll need me to bail you out. How funny you can't remember! If you occasionally forget things, don't worry. It doesn't necessarily mean you're developing Gradual Askalar Neuro-Decay. What you're experiencing is probably perfectly normal.

At least that's what Greta says in her second memoir, *Captive Mind: Sourcing the Self After Askalar.* You should pick it up. It's not doing as well as the first one but you can find it on Amazon.

"Sophomore slump?" Yeah . . . I guess you could call it that . . . in a negative way. But Greta renounced all that concern about getting ahead and ratings and book sales a long time ago. You know she's a real . . . writer. She doesn't really succumb to trends and styles and the fickle marketplace. She moved upstate, since breaking up with Carl, and has a gorgeous place along the river. She's teaching and dating happily. It's a simple life: no TV, no pushy job, no demanding fakery. And I think because she was so open, she met this great simple guy, Bedford, who is a maple syrup farmer and totally devoted to her. He's just not a hipster. He's real.

Oh! Hold the elevator!

Oh wow that sounds so creepy of me, sorry.

Thank you. Oh wow hi Anna! You look AMAZING!

See you honey. I'll call—

THE LOST ONE   by Jacob Fountainhead ™

i saw an old friend the other day
i had not seen in a while
'been through so much in this hard cruel world
so hard for 4 this soul 2 ~~even~~ smile
without a word i heard a story
of pain and of tears
It's the story of the lost One
and the lost one's lost years

The children in the playground
do they really know that
some of them will wander
while some of them will grow
Some will dream a big dream
On top of the jungle gym
while some 'll spin on the carousel
and never stop the spin

Oh have you seen the lost One wandering around
It's sometimes hard to understand the Lost One's weighted
the lost one started out the same   frown
as you and me, you see
But blown with the wind
This little seed ~~was blown~~ drifted into barren land
And landed in the sand.

Settling

a yard sale on an obscure block in the outer borough, 2003

Hello? I saw you from down the block! I wasn't sure if it was you or not because it looked like you were wearing terry-cloth and I couldn't believe that you would ever wear terry-cloth! But then I discover it IS you! How wild! I can't believe how crazy it is to run into you! I love your shirt! How funny!

So this is where you moved. It's a sketchy street but who cares, right? Everyone has said there is such good cheap stuff being sold around this area, so I just came because I need to fill up a few rooms in my beach house. Is—

Cough cough . . . Whooo! That bus was so loud and polluting. I feel sorry for the people on this block.

You live on this block? Oh that building right there? The one with the sort of deep cracks in the foundation? Wow it looks so intimidating from here with the charred façade and scratched wooden doorway. Which is your window?

That one? That one window? It's in the basement. Hey from here it looks like your place is cozy. Cute. Cute 'n' cozy. Perfect for you. Sort of frenchy and disheveled. It fits your granola style. Well roll up your sleeves—looks like you have a LOT of work to do, huh? But I bet you are renting it for a song, right? Can I ask how much?

For THIS? Well in a way I guess that makes sense. I read in *Time Out* that this whole area is right on the brink of becoming more of a community and not a nest of prostitution and crystal meth labs . . . I just didn't know that prices inflated BEFORE a neighborhood was hip. Ugh, I forgot how crazy it is to rent and not own your place. My tenants probably feel tense like you do. But it's so cool you have your own place now. After years of roommates. It's like you are finally adult. A rite of passage at thirty-five! I mean thirty-six!

So what's fer sale? Oh wow. I really like these bathroom window curtains in goofy prints . . . oh I see, they're shorts. Oh man, one of those Ikea standing lamps. Wow that is almost cool again it's so uncool. No wonder you're unloading it. Is anyone even buying it?

A set of knives, some dishware you probably bought upstate, some old ironic board games from the seventies. Look at these shirts! They are from your kooky-baby-tee-club-kid phase, right? Ha! Wow, a million trillion years ago. And your blue baggy painter's pants from college. Wow, I can't believe you held on to this for so long.

So how's work?

Oh wow. That's terrible. Yeah, actually not to freak you out but I kind of heard about what happened.

Well I don't know what they said but I think sexuality is a part of our lives. So what if your Internet sex profile was emailed all over the office? That damn Doctor Faust virus!

Well being fired is so not anything to be embarrassed or humiliated about. I mean if I were you I would be kind of relieved. It was such a demanding job. And some people aren't good under pressure. And then to move here with a brave face. That's so strong-willed of you. You're an inspiration. No really. Like the Liza Minnelli of the new millennium.

I can't believe you found time to pack up and move with all that's happened. Are you OK? Is there anything I can do? It's just that I read all those reports about Askalar, how they are discovering its radically detrimental side effects. And knew you had gone on it in spite of warnings and—

No. You know what? You look great. I think you look amazing. You have matured in your face and I actually prefer you with premature gray!

Wow so many old CDs. You love your music, dontcha? It's funny what people decide to sell. Oh. What's this? Oh MY GOD!! It's Jacob's old band before he hit big, 2 Much! Oh, wait that's right your band too. This is crazy! Four dollars?!?! You could actually make WAY more on eBay, with this, you know. I hope you haven't been just selling a stack of these all day . . .

Sigh. What a pretty day. It must be nice to be outside and enjoy the weather.

Cough cough! Another bus! Cough!

Well, I can't stay too long. I've got so much to do. I'm teaching Pookalan at three, and before that I want to get in a good hour on the Ellipticycle (did you read that CNN.com sidebar article? It's been proven by doctors that a mix of Ellipticycle and other Eastern exercise actually offers better muscle toning and spiritual center-ing than yoga . . . AND it releases proto-morphins in the brain that have antiaging properties! I'm so glad I never really stopped doing the Ellipticycle) and then I gotta pick up Sam who is deep in rehearsals for the lead in this huge new musical-biography rock opera of the life of Van Gogh.

You didn't hear about it? I guess you've been using newspapers to wrap your glassware. Yeah. Everyone is so intrigued by it, and there was a profile of Sam, interviewing him about his process. Just focusing on how an actor builds a character that promises to be a major performance.

And yes, we're still together—he keeps his love life out of the press. Funny—I never in a million years would have thought we would end up together. I'm so embarrassed! It's like a dumb romantic comedy starring Kate Hudson or something! It's so embarrassing!

I don't know, I guess not being all "I need love"-ish actually has made me more confident and ready to receive it? It's the great paradox of life. But, hello! I have you to thank. Just because last time I saw you I was saying something about Sam and you said "Jeez you talk about him like he's your boyfriend," like you were irritated and I thought about it really hard and realized you were right.

No you did say that. Or maybe you just looked at me like you were saying that.

Anyway the next week everything sort of fell into place. He was on the set of *Devil's Dogs* and I called him just to say hi. I was afraid he was too busy, but he appreciated the call. I think the whole war re-creation was getting to him. He was working such long hours, and trying to really get into his role as a U.S. Army Ranger sent to guard a small village of frightened Afghani women against an attack by a terrorist cell. He was sleeping in a mud hut. It was a true re-creation of Afghanistan's desolate, bone-dry landscape, rebuilt up in a lot on the outskirts of Toronto. It's just cheaper there. Sam just sounded different on the phone. It's hard to describe.

Sam knew I really needed some time to recoop after all the press junkets and pressure from my Oscar nomination and so he asked me to join him and Johnny in Laos because they were filming *Boys of Summer 2* there, as you know. It was filmed on Richard Branson's private island. Spectacular, as you probably guessed. Well he kept saying wait till the full moon, wait till the full moon to me, and I was like shut up Sam! Then on the full moon, I was dancing with Johnny's wife Vanessa and their beautiful French children to some hilarious French pop music and Sam motioned to me to come over so I did, and he guided me through the glowing woods to a private lagoon. (As he crept through the woods shirtless I couldn't help but think of him in his role as Pete in *Red Red Wine*! Sexomatic!) We could hear the party revelry far off. It was so bright, the light mixed with the amazing phosphorescent algae in the water, casting undulating, pulsing lines on Sam's chiseled upper body. He had deposited two matching surfboards in the underbrush earlier that day and handed one to me. It was such a warm night, and we treaded water while he reached into his suit and I was like Sam what is up with you, and he just pulled out this HUGE mother of pearl necklace and said, "I got this on my journey through the Mideast. In Kabul, it's a tradition to present this to the individual whom you feel contains part of your *abdabimam*." (It roughly translates to "the fleshiness of the soul.") "I want to marry you," he said, and then almost slipped off his surfboard and I was like, "Hey don't drop that! That's my soul!" Hahahahahahahaha! So . . .

Yeah, we're together. It was hard at first with everyone around us being so freaky. It just takes work to be in a couple. Especially with both our careers rocketing off into the stars at the same time and the whole looks thing, which is so stupid and hard to, you know, deal with, but we had some really really good friends to help us through the, um . . . transition . . . Julia, Meg, Demi, and Ashton have been so so so so wise about it all.

No I would have called you but I didn't want—sometimes you can be—

Anyway, so. He's going through such a transition professionally. Ever since the dumb Oscar thing. It's so difficult at his level, because all he wants to do is act in like one good well-written film a year, which is so hard, because there are really very few roles for classically good-looking men in their thirties, less than you think.

One major moment for me through all of this was we were invited to screen *Devil's Dogs* for George W. Having dinner with the President was an awesome, incredible, once-in-a-lifetime experience, even if I don't think he was legitimately elected.

Oh! We bought a brownstone! Yeah! We take the top two floors and we rent out the first floor and that actually pays for the whole thing. And it gives us enough money left over for us to buy property in the North Fork which we rent out in the winter, and that gives us enough money to—oh you'll love this—buy that incredible place in Costa Rica that you pointed out in *Nest* magazine? You know? The one you always said you'd kill yourself to live in?

Well, we got it!

And Sam is in HEAVEN sanding and rebuilding and renovating. He's such a shy lumberjack kind of guy. He keeps me centered. He's such a homebody.

Speaking of, Carl's helping us build a foundation, pouring cement. You know how good he is with his hands and stuff. He really looks good. Aren't you so excited for his wedding in Provincetown?

You know.

You don't?

Him and Lyle.

Lyle Franklin.

I am so sure you knew! You just probably forgot. He probably didn't have your new address or you would have gotten the invite. Didn't you fill out the change-of-address form? You did? But did you fill it out online? The special green form change-of-address locator E-card? No not the yellow notification form, the GREEN form! Oh yeah, it IS kind of important with everything being processed electronically these days.

Yeah, he and Lyle Franklin are hot and heavy. Carl is finally happy. It sort of makes sense, you know, thinking back to him in college, that he needed someone sort of lighthearted like Lyle.

I was there when they met, at the Millionaire's Club Annual Cookout. The theme was "psycho exes who hang on too long" and Carl was hilarious! They met and it was like magic or something.

Anyway, they want to start a family, and of course the first person they thought of to be the mother was Greta. So they are all—what can I say—making something beautiful happen! It makes me want to cry!

I was with Greta not four months ago and she was so sad. Her book hadn't sold so well, and she had broken up with her boyfriend, and felt so alone. But I told her, Greta, I really believe that the Universe is a living being. Ask of it and it will respond. If you live your life in a loving way it will give you what you need. And so she asked of it, and things turned around for her. Now she's writing about this big spiritual turnaround in her life.

As for ME, I am soo tired . . . I just want to go sit in our surface pool of our renovated orchid farm and lie back and enjoy life. I've just been so up and down lately, up and down. I might be directing a Billy Crystal movie but my heart just isn't in it. It's not a passion project. It's making me re-think the offers I have been getting to produce this kind of major Paramount thrillogy that everyone and their retarded sister is throwing money at, starring Julianne and even though she is, like, the great actress of our time, and I really love her as a person (and love her husband Bart and sometimes baby-sit their kids in their gorgeous Meatpacking District home), I just want to wait a bit until I really feel inspired to work on something more meaningful, you know? Like I would love to just sit like you are and simply unpack my few belongings and try to decorate my one-room studio and just live with everything shaved down and simple again. I'm just so sick of the shiny, glossy, beauty-obsessed world of top-selling pop and the three-dollar-ninety-five-cent mochaccino froth. Sometimes I thank the Lord I have a simple garden that I can walk through and just look at life in its simple organic beauty.

Everything is so lush and green there. Ha! It's weird probably for you to hear me say that I know I mean I'm the LAST person in the world who would think I could actually tend a garden but it turns out I just have this natural green thumb!

I sort of envy you and the hard work you'll have to put in to fix all this. Here you are just starting out again, at thirty-five, buying an ol' meth lab. I wonder how many people died here. So what are you doing for work?

Oh! No! I'm not smirking! It's the bus exhaust. On the contrary, I hear they have really good benefits at Wal-Mart.

Oh you're temping. You're such a free spirit still, it's amazing.

But this would be a good opportunity to really budget your time and find some other skills and make a leap forward. Do something different than your normal "go out on the prowl for love" thing. What about learning some kind of tech or repair work? Or teaching for Stanley Kaplan? Or, I know! An adult internship at the Modern Art Museum. It's sort of for grandmoms who go back to work. You don't need anything. Not even a high school degree, so it's not stressful. I'm on the board there. It doesn't pay, in fact you have to pay for it but I think it's just important for you to keep your mind busy.

This age of our lives. It's weird. I would have never predicted the fates of the Clarkwell College Cabal, you know? Now Tyler is barely around, he's traveling so much going to Biennials and Bienniales. And Sheila's amazing advertising and Internet empire. And Greta, finding solace in writing, developing a real voice. And Carl finally finding happiness. And Sam and me. How we all have all evolved, huh?

We have our careers or we have found love or we have found something like love in some other way, like a house or a pet (I'm so sorry to hear about Checkers by the way!) we've learned to face the facts about our lives, you know? Yeah, all those outsized ambitions have been shattered or realized. For all of us! No matter what! It's weird how we're all just settling down now. Or just settling.

It's just so sad to see people in life so . . . seedless. I mean not like you. You are doing your thing. But there are some people out there who are never satisfied with who they are? Who search and search? Who try to wipe away any feeling of "not having it all" with food, CDs, and self-help books? Who while away their time from meaningless job to meaningless job, fleeting thought to fleeting thought, implausible ideal to implausible ideal, love object to love object? Those people, who always seem to be single and short on cash? And they slightly look like they're going to cry all the time?

Oh wow what a beautiful mirror!

Aw . . . what's this? Your books . . . what are these all? *Keeping an Open Heart in Closed-Off Times, Reason for Hope, Visions of Utopia*, Ruskin, Ginsberg, Patti Smith . . . It's good that you are finding inspiration. It reminds me of my Burning Man phase. It's good for parties.

No, it's good. All that '70s hippie idealism mixed with '90s knee-jerk activism. Those funny lies that our flaming liberal professors told us at Clarkwell. And we watched all of that devolve into dumb politically correct jargon and flaccid politics, right? As if sitting around singing "Kumbaya" and holding hands would ever change anything. Puh-leeze. I'd rather just go to the source—to the holy space my guru Sahatma Yoginanda trained me to find inside myself. And also I like to give three percent of my income to charities.

Aw, look at this—*Free to Be You and Me*. I remember that book. And *Sesame Street!* And an old hardcover of *Where the Wild Things Are*. Wow I can't believe you held on to this stuff.

It's hard to say good-bye to those youthful delusions of poetry. Those moments, as a kid, when you sat in the comfortable crook of a tree root and waited to see an elf or cupped a firefly in your hands one hot August and felt its precious buzz, like the little mindless thing was speaking to you. When you laid back and looked deeply into the sky and thought about infinity and your little heart leapt with possibility. And that feeling came up again when you . . . when we . . . try to build relationships that may be based on youthful idealism and not mutual respect. Like trying to fit your heart into a story that it just wasn't built for. Those love objects that drive you crazy, those super-high-styled ambitions you would never be able to achieve. And if these desperate desires aren't acknowledged through therapy or self-work or yoga or Pookalan, then those outsized dreams bellow out of control and it becomes your atmosphere, you know?

Then, you move to the city, you hope for magic and not adult goals, right? You see the snow quieting a busy street, or the ghostly grind of trash trucks at five in the morning, or you stand on a rooftop at night, looking at the loving throb of lights below. And you feel as if there was somebody winking at you from somewhere? That soon, some avuncular Gepetto will grace you with animated life. That all the goofy swells of hope you've had since you were a kid will be unified with the real and glorious present moment, and you will feel happy, and find that perfect person to take you into his or her arms.

But then, that it doesn't happen, you have that horrible painful moment of realization that all your attempts (with boyfriends or Internet dates or whatever) were a wasted series of synapses in your brain. A complex net of electrical currents. Huge inefficient super-structure. And then with that realization all the signs and symbols begin to flake away like aged paintings.

And everything seems colorless. Everything seems tan and flat. Bleached and refined. A bunch of bar codes and billboards and brightly packaged product. What's the inspiration in all that, right? And nothing is enchanting anymore. And you get on the subway, sitting across from some attractive person and think, "Wow, I used to believe this was my chance at love," and then you realize that there are no such things as chance meetings, no more chance happenings in life, no more chances at all, essentially. Because there is no magic. Because all those childish hopeful happinesses were just in your mind. Those Sesame Street books and colorful Candyland games and Chronicles of Narnia are just objects—just promises that were offered to you, all manufactured for you to believe in them, nothing more. And you sit there, dreamless, worried, deflated, wondering if this is how life ends up— and in, like, under ten years you'll just be wrinkled and sitting in a bay window with a vodka and Clamato looking out over the active traffic on the street, raving to the buses and neighbors and passersby about the noise.

I don't mean you—you. I mean a general You.

This mirror is so beautiful. Are you sure you want to get rid of it? It makes you look so good! See? See? Look in the mirror. Look in the mirror.

What's wrong? This is not your normal voice. Your voice sounds different. Sort of . . . softer . . . like you are whispering in a dark, dark room.

You're not still on Askalar are you?

Yeah. Maybe it's time for you to get some air. Some distance in your life.

Yes . . .

Yes.

ASKALAR LINKED TO MENTAL ISSUES
Found to contain levels of toxic mercury

ASKALAR PULLED FROM SHELVES

The
ly
bee
"G
(G
A:

Masked Heart Trauma and Feelings of Loss Associated with Askalar

The little clear pill, Askalar, originally prescribed for Disorder, has now been linked to severe depression and "Gradual Askalar Neuro-Decay" (GAN), according to reports from the Association for Prescription Pills. Makers of Askalar, the Curckellan Group, have answered the claim that Askalar causes mental instability and probable death with what critics of the drug call "evasion." According to the company, "Curckellan vehemently rejects the claims. We are sorry for the handful of individuals who may be reacting psychosomatically to medical advances. We stand by our drug as a tool promoting mental health and correcting chemical imbalances."

Starting Over

in a remote village tavern on the farmlands of New Zealand, 2004

Breaker! Breaker! Leave that bag of trash alone! Wait it's moving! Breaker, get away from the homeless person!

Oh I'm sorry, how awful. I apologize, sir . . . or ma'am . . . I just thought . . .

Hello? Is that you? How weird. I . . . can't . . . believe it! You're the last person I would expect to see here!

Wait! Come back, it's just me!

Careful! Don't slip on that—

Whup!

Ouch, that must have hurt. Are you OK? Come on, upsy daisy! Yeah, it's hard to get used to the wet climate here. It makes everything so slick. Here, sit down on this bench.

Wow it's so weird that you're here. But I guess it makes sense—everyone and their mother is moving to New Zealand these days after *Lord of the Rings* and all. So let me guess. You're here, trying to start over, getting away from the false fakeness of simulated city life—all that promotion and cruel competition you were sort of sucked into. I'm so glad to see you're getting back to basics after all that bad stuff.

Where do you live? Oh wow—yeah, I heard you can still find some cheap run-down barns in that area. Just be careful, you know. Friends of mine who have remote homes (like a lot of my famous or whatever star-friends) always talk about how there are a lot of hidden dangers to this kind of rustic life. Bad blizzards, snakes, hurricanes, stuck in your barn without any food. And then of course there's the whole threat of losing it . . . you know, the *Apocalypse Now* Syndrome. But I don't think you'll have a problem. You are looking so hearty and ravaged. In a COOL way!

Yeah, we've got a house here, Sam and I. And listen, if you ever need anything, or if you're homesick, you can just trek over to our place. We have a heliport that gets us to the U.S. in about eight hours. We're "bicontinental." Also Sheila and I are opening a chain of organic convenience stores and Pookalan studios in the area next year, so if you can hold out till then, you can—

What? Why are you so upset? What is it? Why are you crying? You poor little strange thing.

No, you can tell me. Don't be shy.

Come on, sweetie. Come on, just let it out.

I know it's hard. I know it's been hard.

But I'll always be by your side. I've known you forever. We've been through so much. You can tell me everything.

I'm your closest friend.

Epilogue

a gathering of friends

Wow. Thank you all for coming here!

First I want to thank Mr. Branson for underwriting travel costs to get everyone here. And I want to thank Avi for this amazing white canopy and candles, and Bobby for his incredible food and Robert who did such amazing floral arrangements. Let's give them all a round of applause! Thank you!

So, well, here we all are. Thank you for coming to this windy point . . . a location that, only two weeks before, was where my best friend's life ended . . . a life we all know, now, was in terrible turmoil.

As the small handful of my best friend's friends, family, and loved ones, you may have thought you knew the inner life of this . . . special child . . . who seemed like such a normal, fine, conversationally competent person. But no, we were wrong.

I actually was the last person to really talk and connect with my best friend. Underneath that uniform, "normal," almost shaky exterior, there was an intense, almost desperate ambition, a paranoia and despondent emotional pain hidden so well from most of you.

We watched our friend yearn for freedom from struggles with work and love—struggles and life-snags that just seem like surmountable obstacles to most of us. We watched helplessly as our friend—unemployed and loveless—left a fine, plain life behind and moved to this isolated, harsh countryside, where there is no escape from the battering elements upon a vulnerable, unexercised body. And upon an unstable mind.

In many ways, my best friend's life almost echoed the anxiety of a generation: Disillusioned. Debt-ridden. Obsessive. Tired.

My best friend felt somehow not good enough, not thin enough, not successful enough. Riddled with Disorder that was never adequately treated.

Perhaps that is why our friend stepped outside of more "successful" choices in college—bewilderingly majoring in Folk and Myth. Where others of us have made films, hosted TV shows, written novels, our friend kept trying to join mankind's wonderful historical tapestry. Sad and futile attempts to be a recognized person in the world left our friend feeling challenged and beleaguered.

If nothing else, my best friend was just that . . . a "challenged soul."

Which is why I decided to start the My Best Friend Fund for Challenged Souls. To provide support and grants to creatively lost individuals who make bad choices. We will be having our first benefit gala at Lotus next month. Hosted by Adrien Brody, Pink, and Heidi Klum—all whom never knew our friend (how would they have crossed paths?), but after I have talked to them, feel as if they did.

And we at the My Best Friend Fund have some great news!

I have just received word that we will be receiving a special Filmmaker Seed Grant from Sheila Nevins herself, the executive producer over at HBO, to make a docudrama about my best friend's mundane yet terrible life. And actually Sofia will be directing, who is here today! Where is she . . . ? Why don't you stand up, Sofia?

And Sam, my man, my most talented man, will be playing the lead. Already he is deep in the role, gaining thirty pounds, and we'll be using the latest equipment, putting latex on his face to create age spots and acne and wrinkles.

I think you all would agree that my best friend would be happy that my life was finally clicking in place. Isn't it ironic that it took death to make it happen?

But for now, let's all have a moment of silence, as we scatter the ashes of this challenged soul, who now may finally be happy and free to wander aimlessly in the air.

Good-bye my sweet, discouraged, troubled friend. Death be not proud.

Oh. Sorry. I'm not sure if we captured that on film, so if you don't mind I am just going to repeat myself:

Good-bye my sweet, discouraged, troubled friend. Death be not proud.

ACKNOWLEDGMENTS

Thank you

Tina Bennett   Colin Dickerman

Lisa Archambault   Gary Baura
Tessa Blake   Nora Burns
Nell Casey   Cary Curran
Susan Dominus   Carl James Ferrero
Everyone at Fez   Daisy Garnett
Casey Greenfield   Gregg Guinta
Murray Hill   David Ilku
Ariel Kaminer   Amanda Katz
Svetlana Katz   Lucinda Rosenfeld
Viva Ruiz   Maria Russo
Anna Catherine Rutledge   David Samuels
David Schweizer   Larry Shea
Pam Lawrence Svendsen   Lorraine Tobias

And thanks to Robert Jones—we miss you.

A NOTE ON THE AUTHOR

Mike Albo is a writer and performer who lives and
loves in Brooklyn. He has performed his comedic
monologues (co-written with his longtime friend
Virginia Hefferman) all over the country and abroad,
in cities including Los Angeles, San Francisco,
New York, Toronto, and London. His first
novel, *Hornito*, was published by HarperCollins
in 2000. His Web site is www.mikealbo.com.

A NOTE ON THE TYPE

The text of this book is set in Bembo. This type was first
used in 1495 by the Venetian printer Aldus Manutius
for Cardinal Bembo's *De Aetna*, and was cut for
Manutius by Francesco Griffo. It was one of the types
used by Claude Garamond (1480–1561) as a model
for his Romain de L'Université, and so it was the
forerunner of what became standard European type
for the following two centuries. Its modern form
follows the original types and was designed for
Monotype in 1929.